THE HEIRLOOM OBSESSION

ORLA KELLY PUBLISHING

SD Saunders

Dedication

To my sister and best friend Lin, for all the brainstorming and helpful advice you give me. Without you I would never have written this story. Thanks for believing in me.

In memory of my Grandad, George Arthur Crow, who served his country in the RAF during WW2, shot down and killed in his Beaufighter over the Bay of Biscay. His body was never recovered.

28/02/1922 – 13/08/1944

'Like so many other service men, gone but never forgotten'.

Contents

Prologue

June 7ᵗʰ 1952

Christina fingered the heavy emerald gem necklace around her throat; it felt cold against her skin, the main square cut emerald, flanked on either side by smaller emeralds and diamonds hung in a stunning fan display across her chest. Her heavy silk gold ball gown made her feel sophisticated, the blue green delicate embroidered flowers complimenting the emeralds as if made to be worn together. The tight bodice and nipped in waist, giving Christina a tiny figure, the full skirts flaring out over her slender hips. A glance in her vanity mirror revealed the sparkle of the step cut gems, her heart shaped face staring back, blonde hair swept up in a rather grownup chignon. Her full cupid's bow mouth slightly open, green eyes sparkling with excitement over the upcoming party her parents Lord and Lady Trafford were holding for her eighteenth birthday, she could not believe that after months of planning it was finally here, and she was wearing the heirloom emerald necklace.

She hoped Jack would be there; he had sent her a note saying to unlock the French doors in the library for him to slip in from the garden to rendezvous at 8pm, and as she re-read the note, she felt her excitement grow. She knew her parents would not approve. "Young heiresses don't get involved with stable boys", her father had admonished several times over this past summer, but still Christina hoped Jack could be persuaded to stay at the party. Staring again at the necklace, she felt an uneasy feeling stir inside; this was the Trafford emerald necklace, its worth priceless, its history endless. It had been in her family for generations, her mother was given this necklace on her wedding day, and now it was hers.

Her cousin Philip felt it was their right to have it as his father James had always made it known; a bone of contention with her uncle who had wanted, in fact expected it as his right, for his wife Isabela to have received it. But tradition was what it was; it only got handed down to the females of the family, and with no daughters, Philip's grandmother, a rather astute lady had realised that her first son's wife, a rather selfish woman, would have had the necklace reset and modernised. So she had instead decided to hand it down to Christina's mother Elise, a much gentler old fashioned girl, who had married her second born son Edward, and who would be far wiser, and more in keeping with tradition.

Christina felt flushed; she had been dancing all evening. Glancing at the ballroom clock, she noted the time; only fifteen minutes before she would see Jack. Slipping away, she made her way down the corridor, all evening she had felt uncomfortable, a feeling she could not shake. Stepping into her father's study, she unclasped the emerald necklace;

maybe if she took it off and put it somewhere safe, she could enjoy what was left of the evening. Having made her mind up, and with the necklace now stowed safely away, Christina slipped out of the study and feeling much lighter, headed to the library.

Pushing the heavy library door ajar, Christina slipped into the darkened room, with only the moonlight from the French doors leading to the garden, lighting her way. She carefully made her way silently across the thick pile carpet, towards the double doors. Thankfully, the heavy velvet curtains, hanging on each side remained open. Unlocking the doors, Christina felt a frisson of excitement, as she would soon see Jack. Stepping back, she felt rather than saw a presence; someone was behind the curtain, uncertainly she held her breath. The man's arm shot out and an intense pain exploded on Christina's temple; clutching at Jack's note, Christina sank to the floor. As blackness started to envelop her, she could feel the figure leaning over her, the smell of whisky on his breath making her nauseous, his voice nothing but a harsh whisper, "damn it girl! Where is the necklace". The last thing she heard as she succumbed to the blackness.

Chapter 1

Present day

May 13th 2012

I t was a bright sunny morning as Melody drove her car into the designated parking field, where the car boot sale was being held. Men in hi-visibility jackets were directing the steady stream of cars into parking spaces. Having finally claimed her space, and making sure she made a mental note where she was parked, Melody cut the engine. Glancing into the back seat at Toby, her 4 year old golden retriever, seemed to be bursting with excitement. "Ok boy, nearly time", she laughed as his tail swished back and forth, his tongue licking the car window expectantly. It had been their ritual for the last two months, bright and early each Sunday morning, attending these fairs. It was an Aladdin's cave of treasures for Melody's craft shop and the vintage clothes at bargain prices for Melody to re-design was too good to be resisted, along with other odds and ends which would end up in the shop for sale, or in the display window. "Maybe we'll find some treasures today, ay boy", Melody laughed as she let Toby free from the car. Grabbing her tote bag, she said, "let's go".

The walk to the stalls was a short five minutes. Toby was running ahead sniffing the air, delighting in the food smells as different vendors heated up their produce. It was going to be a busy day today; the car park was already filling up. Shoppers milled around the stalls, each one boasting even more items to be picked through than the last. Rifling through the bric-a-bracs, looking for a treasure or two was a great way to spend a Sunday morning. Smiling to herself, Melody could almost hear her loyal employee Susie tutting, "What treasure did you get from the boot fair this time? Another ornament for the shop?" As Melody would produce yet another trinket for displaying in the window.

Susie had been a godsend, working with Melody to bring Simple Crafts, to a successful business entity. At 61, Susie had been looking for a new challenge, something to get her out of the house and from under her retired husband Dave's feet, and had happened upon the shop one morning while out shopping. The card in the shop window had caught her eye, "help wanted" and on that wintery morning, Melody had happily taken Susie on and never looked back. They had instantly felt a comradery, and Susie had taken Melody under her motherly wing. Remembering that day with fond memories, when Susie had walked into the shop. At 5 foot 4 inches, she was a force to be reckoned with, short cropped blonde curly hair, her blue eyes sparkling with mischief. "I've come about the shop assistant job, and to be honest I was going crazy stuck at home with my newly retired husband constantly fussing over me". Melody had warmed to her teasing banter in an instant.

"Everything in that box is for only a pound luv", a rather gruff voice stated, pulling Melody out of her reverie. Bringing her attention back to the box she had been rifling through. A pair of ornate silver-coloured scissors caught her eye; the handles shaped as a peacock's head and body, the blade its tail. The enamel turquoise and blue of the head and body glinted in the morning sunshine. These would look great featured in the shop window, she decided digging into her tote bag. Finding her purse, she pulled out a pound coin, and handed it to the market stall guy.

"Want me to wrap them for you, luv", he bellowed, already eyeing his next customer.

"No thanks", Melody smiled back at him, dropping them into her bag. Pleased with her find, she started to move off, only to catch sight of Toby ambling towards her with a big purple plush toy dangling from his mouth, with a rather triumphant look on his face. "Now who do I have to pay for that Tob's?" She laughed as she ruffled his head. It had been Toby's game every time they came to a boot fair; he would run off and hunt for a soft toy returning with his prize and a stall owner in hot pursuit. Glancing around, she soon saw three stalls away the stall owner waving at her. Making her way over with Toby at her heels, she paid him for the plush toy, who today was fortunately good humoured about it; some did not always possess a sense of humour.

"I think it's time for a little break aye, Tob's, want a drink". They headed towards one of the less crowded burger vans. Melody ordered a can of cola and a bottle of water, then headed over to the seats provided by the refreshment stand. Pulling out Toby's collapsible water bowl from her bag, an over enthusiastic Toby started lapping the streaming water as she poured it. "Can't wait, aye Toby", she laughed, placing the bowl on the floor. She settled back into her chair and took a large gulp of her cola; as the cola's fizz exploded in her mouth, Melody blinked back tears. "I'm just as bad as you Tob's, we both need to slow down".

Sitting there people watching, Melody considered what stalls to browse next. The boot fair was getting busier by the moment, the sun's rays gently warming her face. Reaching into her bag, Melody pulled out her compact mirror, her hazel eyes with flecks of amber and green stared back at her. Dabbing the powder across her face, she tried in vain to hide the sprinkling of freckles across her nose and cheek bones; she had never liked her freckles, she thought wrinkling her nose at her reflection. Pulling her heavy golden curls off her hot neck, she secured it tightly into a ponytail.

Now she felt ready for more bargain hunting. Dropping her compact back into her bag, she leaned down and gave Toby a rub; he rolled over showing his belly.

"Can I stroke him please", Melody looked up to see a little girl smiling at her and Toby, her mother smiling her approval.

"Of course you can", Melody said as she smiled back. Having gained her confidence, the little girl squatted down beside Toby and began rubbing his belly.

"What's his name?" The little girl now demanded with an infectious grin.

"His name is Toby, and he loves a belly rub", Melody answered while Toby took delight in his new found friend.

"Mummy, can we have a dog", the little girl asked in a very small voice.

"Maybe one day", she sighed, "now thank the lady and let's go find your dad". Melody said goodbye to them both, scooping up Toby's bowl and emptying the remaining water, folded it and put it back into her bag. Dropping her soda can into the trash bin, she tapped her leg. "Come on Tob's, time to shop", and they headed back to the stalls.

As she browsed, Toby ran back and forth, sniffing anything that took his fancy, his toy dangling from his mouth. She loved simple days like this and trekking back and forth to the car with her purchases ensured Toby had a lot of exercise for the day. She stopped walking, looking around at how far they had gone, glancing along the stalls, she saw the one stall she had been looking for. Mick ran this stall and had always got something of interest for her.

"Morning Melody", Mick shouted as she approached, "I've been looking out for you".

Melody smiled. "Hi Mick, any treasures for me today?"

"Well today's your lucky day. I have an old vintage trunk, filled with some old dresses, I'm sure you could work your magic on", he winked, guiding her over to the back of the stall. "The wife said not to bother with bringing them today, but I was sure you'd like the materials". She carefully lifted the lid, a heavy gold silk gown sat folded on top with blue green delicately embroidered flowers scattered over it.

Moving it slightly out of the trunk, some places on the gold gown were slightly faded, showing that it was old.

Further into the trunk, other gowns lay folded. "I'd give you the trunk and contents for £20", Mick bantered bringing Melody back to his presence.

"How about £15 Mick"? Melody knew this was more than fair, she wanted this trunk and the material of at least the first dress; she knew it would make a lovely party dress for her niece Lucy, who was turning six next month. She had promised to make her a party dress, and this would be perfect; the blue green embroidered flowers in the gown were Lucy's favourite colour and would match Lucy's green eyes.

"Oh, you drive a hard bargain Melody, but I can't haul it back home with me, so it's yours", Mick laughed, clicking the latches back, and checking that the trunk was now secure. Melody paid Mick, and laughed off another customer's offer to carry it over to her car.

"Thanks, but I'm sure I can manage just fine", leaving the stall and the helpful customer. She gripped the handle, and made her way back for the fourth time that day across the field to her car.

He watched the girl and her dog as she wandered slowly across the green between the stalls, the trunk she was carrying seeming to make her way hard. He was sure it was one of the trunks he had been on the lookout for. He swore as he ground his cigarette out on the floor; he had nearly gained that last trunk, but as fate would have it, had lost out as he had just been minutes behind her. An offer from him to carry it for her had met with a sweet smile and a firm but dismissive, "I'm good, thank you". Still thinking that he could just make off with it in this busy boot fair, was not one of his finest ideas, he would just have to think of another way. "Damn", he swore again, it was not his day today. Lighting another cigarette, he followed her keeping a safe distance, stopping every now and again pretending to look at what the stalls had to offer to keep any suspicious eyes at bay. He watched as she stopped at the boot of a little red Renault Clio; unlocking the car, she lifted the boot and carefully placed the trunk inside. He would just have enough time to make it to his van; following her home was now his only option.

A rather rotund woman crashing into him brought his focus back to where he was standing. "Oh excuse me", she nervously laughed as her bags of purchases fell to the ground. Feeling more than a little annoyed, he stooped down to help retrieve the bags. "I was so busy trying to keep an eye on my little Jimmy, I didn't see you there", she breathlessly explained, her eyes darting around anxiously until coming to rest on a little boy two stalls over, playing with toy cars. "Jimmy!" she shrilled as she made her way to the uninterested little boy. Taking a pull of his cigarette, his focus returned to the red Renault and the woman he was following. To his now growing annoyance, the space where her car had been was now empty; his day could not get any worse; he growled low in his throat, "damn it to hell". Quickly walking to his van, he decided that he still had to retrieve all the Trafford estate trunks. "I'm not going to fail on this last one", even if it only looked like it contained bloody evening dresses! He needed another plan and fast.

Melody manoeuvred her car out of the now busy boot fair's makeshift car park, her eyes sparkling at the thought of the trunk she had just purchased. The trunk itself would make a particularly good window display, but the real treasure was the heavy silk gold gown, stored within. Plans of how she would transform it into the party dress for Lucy flew through her mind, the blue green embroidery would look great with some matching tulle and ribbons. It would be perfect, and she had four weeks to finish it; she had plenty of time. She could not wait to get started on it, but first she had to swing by her shop. Some of her purchases needed dropping off into the back room, where she would sort them out Monday morning.

Pulling into her space in the empty car park at the back of her shop, Melody let Toby out of the car. "Stretch your legs, Tob's", Melody told her dog, glancing over her shoulder as she let herself into the shop and disarmed the alarm. Toby ran back and forth, chasing crows, barking in delight as they took flight. Balancing a cardboard box on her hip, Melody flicked the light switch on. It was dark in the storeroom, even with the lights on, the shelves groaning with all odds and ends of craft wares. Making her way to the far wall, she placed the box down; "Two more to go", she muttered, feeling pleased with all of her purchases that morning.

Ten minutes later, with the last of the cardboard boxes full of craft bits stacked against the back wall in the storeroom, Melody rubbed her hands together with glee. It had been a good day; she would have plenty of things to fill the shop shelves.

Setting the alarm and locking up, she made her way back to the car, the bright sunshine causing her to squint. "Jump in Tob's", she coaxed. Securing him safely inside, she climbed into the driver's seat. All she needed now was to get home and have a coffee and put her tired feet up. A lovely Sunday afternoon pouring over the trunk and its contents and designing Lucy's party dress beckoned to her as she pulled out of the car park. Melody smiled to herself, today was turning out to be quite perfect.

Chapter 2

Melody pulled up outside her home, the little cottage just outside of town, which was her sanctuary; it had recently been left to her by her late grandmother. The garden now in full bloom, made her smile once more to herself, a variety of colours welcomed her. She had loved to play here as a child, fond memories of sunny days with her grandmother working in the garden always held a special place in her heart.

As she opened her front gate, she moved the heavy trunk to her other hand and slowly made her way to the front door. She noticed a white van drive slowly out of the cul-de-sac; strange for delivery vans to be here on a Sunday, she thought, as she retrieved her key and slid it into the lock.

The heavy red door swung open, and Toby rushed past her with his purple plush toy hanging from his mouth, heading straight down the hall to the kitchen and his bed to play with his latest prize. Placing the trunk just inside the door, she pushed the front door closed. Following Toby down the hall to the kitchen and flicking the coffee machine on, she strolled to the front room to check her answering machine. The red light blinked one new message repeatedly at her; it was probably just Sarah her sister checking up on her. "First a coffee, before I deal with you", she mumbled to herself, deciding a coffee was exactly her next priority.

Having poured a steaming cup of coffee, Melody took a seat at the big kitchen table placed in the centre of the kitchen; it was just the same as her grandmother had left it. Memories of sitting here with her grandmother, helping her with a sewing project or chatting about her day whilst tasting her latest batch of cookies filled Melody with an overwhelming sense of loss. She could almost hear her grandmother's voice telling her about the gardening she had been doing. Smiling, she noted the small vase of flowers from the garden sitting on the table, a tradition of her grandmother's that she still enjoyed doing. "Flowers are blooming well this year, gran", she sighed.

She stole a contented look around the kitchen; the big windows above the sink dominated the room, letting in the afternoon sunshine, bathing everything in a homely glow. Old floral curtains hung on each side of the windows, a lone pot plant the only item on the windowsill. Once, it would have been crammed full of pots with an array of cuttings her grandmother so fondly loved to grow, the memory making her smile sadly. Turning her attention elsewhere, she spied the various plates and mismatched crockery displayed on her grandmother's large kitchen dresser, standing tall beside the old utility doorway and the hall door. Glancing at the old backdoor, where the sun was pouring in through the glass panels highlighting the chipped and peeling paint, and making a mental note to add that chore to her growing list of things to do, she sighed. The large double doors leading from the kitchen to the front room was almost always wedged open and made the area feel open-planned and bright. Maybe a lick of paint in there would be a good start, she mused gazing into the front room at the dingy magnolia walls.

She had lived here for eight months now, and it was still mostly decorated as her grandmother had left it. Not having the heart to change the look of her grandmother's well-loved home, but maybe it was time she gave it her own touch.

Watching absent-mindedly as Toby lay in his bed by the back door snuffling the toy, every now and then raising his head to check she was still there with him. "It's okay boy, I'm still here", she reassured him taking a sip of her coffee. Reaching for her bag, Melody pulled out the ornate silver peacock scissors she had purchased from the boot fair; these really would look good in her new window display. She had a few peacock feathers in the storeroom, and some beads and silks that would make for a stunning display. As she sat formulating her plans for the shop window, Toby let out an excited yap; looking up, Melody saw the back door swing open.

"Hi Mel, it's only me", Alex announced as he walked in. Dropping his basket of vegetables onto the table, he reached down and ruffled Toby's head.

Alex had moved into the cottage next door shortly after Melody had moved in; they had struck up a fast friendship. She learned that he had established a second branch of his successful security company Knight & Brooks with his best friend, Joel Brooks, situated in the heart of town, and by all accounts it was doing well. He had been looking for a new start and a quieter way of life, having been widowed two years earlier, and had finally realised that life in the big city held no sway for him anymore. His quickly learned vegetable gardening and odd job skills had been enjoyed by them both; he had helped Melody with several jobs around her home.

"I thought you might like a few early veggies for some of your delicious soup making", Alex grinned to himself, he was sure of getting an invite to partake of Melody's meal later that evening.

Melody watched as Alex unloaded the freshly picked vegetables onto the draining board. At six foot three, he seemed to fill Melody's small kitchen, his denim jeans clung lovingly to his muscled legs and tight bottom, his t-shirt pulled tight over his broad shoulders, his dark brown hair worn just a little too long in a slick back undercut style, still damp from his shower. His grey blue eyes had been the first thing that had caught Melody's attention, when he had first introduced himself as her new neighbour.

It was now becoming a habit, having Alex appear at her back door with armfuls of produce, or his tools to fix something she had not realised needed fixing. "Well", Alex stood, looking expectantly at her.

Blushing to her roots, Melody realised she'd been caught staring at him. "Sorry, what did you say".

"Think the veggies here pass muster"? Alex repeated, grinning, his eyes sparkling at her blush.

"Oh yes, they are great, you must come over tonight to try them, I was going to make a roast chicken, if you'd like"?

Alex reached out his hand and tucked a stray curl behind her ear. "Sounds lovely Mel, want me back around six"? Melody held her breath, her heart beating excitedly; she wanted him more than he knew.

"Six is great; I have a few things to sort out before then, so that should give me plenty of time".

"Six it is then", he grinned making his exit; as he left Melody sat staring at the back door.

"He really should come with a health warning", she muttered, looking at Toby who seemed to be missing him too. "Now enough daydreaming, time to deal with my answerphone", she chastised herself firmly, rinsing her coffee mug and putting it on the draining board.

The call to her sister Sarah had been a long one; her brief message on the answerphone was just as Melody suspected, Sarah was calling to check if she was ok. Stretching her shoulders, Melody decided if there was one thing her sister could do, it was to talk for Britain! She had agreed to call in and see her the following week with Toby. Melody, for what seemed like the hundredth time, insisted she was fine and didn't need anything. Sarah did seem to worry since her grandmother had died, now that she lived alone out in the countryside; the fact that it was only a ten-minute drive from town, not really registering with Sarah. Reassuring her that she would bolt the doors at night, and that Toby was on guard seemed to calm her sister down.

Talk of Lucy's party dress and the fabric she had bought consumed the rest of the conversation. Wearily, Melody replaced the phone. Glancing at her watch, she let out a sigh; a quick look through the trunk, and then she would have to start preparing dinner.

Placing the old trunk on the kitchen table, Melody ran her hand lovingly over the lid. She fingered the faded gold lettering CET. "I wonder who you belonged to", she mused aloud, noting the many scuffs the old trunk bore. The brown leather trunk was in need of restoration.

"A little leather, oil and you'll be good as new", she sighed. Releasing the latches, she slowly raised the lid. Here in her sunny kitchen, the contents seemed to be almost bursting out, the deep gold of the gown almost looking like a rich honey colour; lifting it out, she placed it carefully over the back of a kitchen chair. The tight bodice cut with a sweetheart neckline, and puffed capped sleeves, with a dropped waist, the full skirts flaring out at the hip, the delicate blue green embroidered flowers twining around the dress, a vast contrast to the gold material.

Reaching back into the trunk to retrieve the next dress, Melody's fingers brushed onto something hard underneath it. She pulled back the dress and folded into its skirts, sat a cloth bag. Reaching out to it, she slipped it from the folds, tipping its contents onto the table; she watched as three old brown leather-bound books, and two letters tied neatly with a red silk ribbon tumbled out. Reaching for one of the books, she looked at the inscription, in the same flowy script that was on the trunk. She saw the initials CET, the other two books held the same identical gold script initials.

Opening the book, the first page looked aged and was yellowing around the edges. Scrawled across the page, was a name penned in black ink in flowy handwriting "Journal of Christina Elizabeth Trafford, 1952". Melody felt a frisson of excitement; turning the page for the first entry, Melody held her breath, a feeling of trespassing into someone's life left her feeling uncertain. Shaking off this absurd feeling, she decided to read the page. After all, this was her property now, she had every right to read it.

"June 9th, 1952

"Today, father and mother have presented me with this rather nice journal. They want to give me a chance to capture my thoughts, in aid of me regaining my memories. I still have no memory of my eighteenth birthday party, which was held for me two days ago, or indeed the weeks leading up to it. No-one is permitted to divulge any information on my lost days, as per our doctor's instructions. Even the staff is avoiding me. They are all treating me like a fragile invalid, and it is all I can do not to let my temper go! I have been delegated to my room while I recuperate; the lump on my head is still unsightly and very tender. Mother thinks it wise for me to keep a low profile; they have invited my younger cousin Primrose to stay and keep me company. I wouldn't mind but we have never been close. She is only thirteen and I've always found her to be a cold, spoilt child, but mother insists it will be good for me and I can find no good excuse to refuse. In a few days, I will try to persuade father into letting me take a walk in the gardens. I shall make a detour and go to the stables to try and see Jack; maybe

he can help me recall some of my missing memories. A rather strange mood seems to have descended over the household. I am quite certain I have heard raised voices from downstairs on more than one occasion". Christina.

Melody sat down onto the kitchen chair, placing the journal on the table, its un-folding story holding her mind in rapture. If only she had time to read more, but she had so much to do. Unpacking the rest of the trunk's contents, Melody smiled to herself. "Well Christina, you really had good taste in clothes". Taking the four gowns through to her craft room, Melody hung three of them onto her clothes rail. She would decide what to do with them later, although the rose-pink one with tiny rosebuds around the satin bodice neckline and a few on the front of the full tulle skirt hem held her gaze; the thought of trying it on and wearing it an exciting prospect. The gold gown she placed onto her mannequin; she would start unpicking the seams of that dress tomorrow, to prepare it for making Lucy's party dress.

Gathering up the remainder of the trunk's contents, Melody made her way to the front room and placed the journals and letters inside the bureau; she would get back to reading them later, she promised herself. Taking the trunk, she pushed it behind one of her grandmother's over-stuffed sofas, which was situated in front of the front room window. She would retrieve it tomorrow to take to the shop for her latest window display. Lastly, she looked at the porcelain doll, still wrapped up in an old shawl; this she placed onto the matching overstuffed floral armchair, arranging the shawl so now its face looked out into the room.

"I bet you have stories to tell", she muttered, casting the doll one last look before heading into the kitchen to prepare dinner.

After showering and slipping into a comfortable pair of jeans and soft white cotton t-shirt, Melody sat at her dressing table. Pulling her Blonde curls into a high ponytail and applying a little mascara and some rose pink lip gloss, she looked once again at her reflection. Satisfied with her attempt, she decided to leave her freckles untouched, and headed once more for the kitchen.

Leaving the back door open after letting Toby out into the garden, Melody checked on the vegetables; pulling down Toby's food bowl, she emptied some left-over pasta into it and mixed in a scoop of kibble. As the kibble poured into the bowl, Toby came racing in from the garden, skidding to a stop on the rough tiled floor.

"Toby sit", she commanded, as he happily obeyed; she placed his bowl down next to his water. "Take", she smiled as his face disappeared into his food, snuffling and crunching his food as his tail wagged back and forth.

"Something smells good", Alex announced as he stepped into the kitchen from the back door. "I brought us some chilled white wine to go with dinner". Holding out the bottle for Melody to inspect, he leaned in closer to her.

"Oh a chardonnay, my favourite, let me get some glasses". Brushing past Alex, she reached up to the overhead cupboard and produced two wine glasses.

Alex pulled the cork screw out of the draw. "Shall I pour"? She looked across at Alex, his lopsided smile made her heart flutter. They had been dancing around each other for months now with easy banter and a mutual attraction; she just was not sure who would make the first move. He was everything she wanted in a man but knowing he had only been a widower for two years, kept her from crossing the line of friendship; what if he was not ready. She would hate to make their friendship awkward. At 34 years old, she knew Alex was happy with his situation. He was finally settling in next door, maybe she could nudge their relationship forward soon.

Melody handed him the glasses. "Sure, why don't you take them and make yourself comfortable in the front room, I'll just check the dinner and follow you in". Alex strolled into the front room and after pouring two glasses of wine, he placed the wine bottle onto the coffee table, settling himself onto the couch. He watched Melody through the wide-open double doors of the front room as she opened the oven to check on the roast. Even in jeans and a plain t-shirt, she got his pulse racing; how long would she keep him at arm's length. He had not been looking for romance when he had moved out of the city, but he felt pleased it had seemed to have found him, he hoped.

From Melody's golden blonde curls to her fluffy penguin slippers, he knew she was perfect for him. He had lost count how many times he had longed to kiss her sweet full lips, sometimes watching her as she puzzled over something and absent-mindedly bit her lower lip. He had never thought he would feel this way again after his wife had died, but time had healed his broken heart and since meeting Melody, he had felt his heart stirring to life again.

At her young age of twenty-six, he knew she had shared the pain of loss also; with her parent's sudden death only a few short years ago in tragic circumstances, and more recently with her grandmother's passing, he knew it had left her reeling and lost. This mutual loss had bonded them over the past few months.

"Everything okay Alex"? Looking up, he smiled at her; she was hesitating in the doorway.

Alex grinned. "I was just wondering Mel, what's with the scary doll"? He pointed at the chair opposite.

Melody sank down onto the sofa next to him; taking a large gulp of her wine, she turned to face Alex. "I found it in a trunk I bought at the boot fair today, along with some incredibly old gowns and some journals. I'm considering giving it to my niece Lucy".

Alex reached his hand out and stroked a finger down Melody's cheek. "You did huh, don't you think it might scare her"?

"What's so scary about a porcelain doll? I think she's quite pretty".

"It's the eyes, Mel, they seem to follow you everywhere". As if on cue, Toby let out a menacing growl; looking up, they saw him stalking up to the chair eyeing the doll, his hackles up.

"Oh, you two are as bad as each other", Melody laughed, rising from the sofa and scooping up the doll. "Let me save you both and put her away". Wrapping the shawl around the face of the doll, Melody put her in the writing compartment of the bureau. "Now, are you both satisfied"? Melody teased rolling her eyes.

Alex reached up and pulled her down onto the sofa with him. "No", he growled pulling her into his embrace. Melody reached up and put her hand on his face, feeling his strong jaw, rough to the touch, his stubble grazing her fingers, the heady smell of his aftershave and soap still lingering. Looking into his piercing grey blue eyes, she felt drawn to him; holding onto his arms, she could feel his muscles flex. As they kissed, she felt herself melting into him. It felt so right, the passionate kiss was all she dreamed it would be; dinner was all but forgotten.

Melody walked around, checking the house was all locked and secure for the night, still dazed about the kisses she and Alex had shared. He had helped her salvage the dinner and even helped with the washing up. They had not spoken about the kiss, but had now both acknowledged their mutual attraction; easy banter had resumed much to her relief. Promising to call in after work the next day, Alex had left late that evening. The kiss goodbye had been almost tender with a promise of more to come.

Checking that Toby was settled in for the night, Melody headed for the stairs and bed; stopping on the first stair she remembered the journals. Reaching the bureau, she pulled out the letters and one journal. Pulling the writing compartment down, she retrieved the porcelain doll and smiling to herself at the thought of Alex's comment about the doll looking scary, she headed up to bed.

Glancing around her bedroom, she felt pleased once again at her decision to make this room her own. The walls now painted the lightest shade of lemon looked warmer in the light from her lamps on her newly purchased white scroll legged bedside tables, her matching dressing table and stool seemed to fit in so well with the old cottage style bedroom. The curtains were now drawn, revealing the dainty forget-me-not flowers in a watercolour style pattern. The material she had purchased from her first car boot fair, she had had enough of the material leftover to cover her dressing table stool too. It still gave her pleasure to know she had made good use of her sewing skills; this really was starting to feel like home.

The box room to the back of the cottage where she had always stayed when visiting her grandmother was now repurposed as a storeroom. It was now crammed full of the old furniture from her new room, and items she still had found no place for. The thought of entering her grandmother's old room was still too much for her to deal with. "One day soon", she sighed, for now, it would remain locked. Placing her clothes into the clothes hamper, Melody smoothed her hand down her silk pyjamas, curling her toes into the thick pile cream carpet. She glanced towards her bed, the white antique metal frame of the double bed contrasting against the forget-me-not blue of the duvet cover and pillows. A contented sigh escaping her lips, Melody grabbed the journal and letters from her bedside table. After propping the pillows on top of one another and turning off one lamp, she slipped into her bed, pulling the duvet over her knees and gently thumbing open the journal.

19th June, 1952

"I am distraught! My walk in the gardens today has left me in shock; my plan to detour my walk to the stables was a success. I was able to slip away from Primrose, and upon arriving at the stables, things took a turn for the worst. I was informed by Tom, the senior stable hand that Jack no longer works for us. No explanations where offered, he could not even say where Jack had gone. I enquired casually from father at this bizarre situation. He seemed quite angry, shutting the conversation down immediately, stating that I was not to speak of Jack again! I feel sure Jack would not just have left without seeking me out first to let me know. If only I could remember, something feels strange about this situation, only I just cannot comprehend what. My headache has returned, I think I shall lie down till it passes. Tomorrow, I will again attempt to unlock my memories; a visit to the ballroom downstairs where my party was held may help me remember". Christina.

20th June, 1952

"Father and mother had to go to town for the morning. With them safely out of the way and Primrose distracted in the library, I decided to take the opportunity to visit the ballroom. As soon as I stepped into the room, a feeling captured my thoughts, like ghosts dancing through my mind just out of reach. Music and dancing, the guests twirling around, a riot of colourful gowns and men in tuxedos, waiters hovering with

trays of champagne and someone watching me, but as I tried to concentrate, the images evaporated like steam in the air. Snatches of the memory of my gold gown flitted through my mind. I ran back to my room to look for it, hoping it would bring more memories flooding back, but after a thorough search through my wardrobes, it strangely became apparent that it was missing. If it had been sent away for cleaning, I am certain it would have been returned by now. I decided I would head down to fathers study to look for any other clues as to what is going on. After looking on and around the desk, I observed that the key had been left in the lock of the draw. Upon opening it, underneath several uninteresting papers and bills, I discovered a note. It was addressed to me from Jack, in sweeping script dated the night of my party. It requested me to unlock the French doors in the library for Jack to slip in unnoticed, for us to meet. I must admit my heart did leap at those few words; he was going to meet me. I slipped the note inside my dress and after re-locking the draw, headed back to my room. I am now convinced this note was why father was so angry when I enquired of Jack, and why he had fired him. Oh, it's such a mess! Will I ever get my blasted memories back".
Christina.

Melody closed her eyes, the journal falling softly from her fingers, her dreams filled with images of bright coloured ball gowns and distinguished suited men and waiters offering overflowing champagne. As she twirled around the ballroom in the rose pink ball gown, laughter filled the air, a dark shadowy figure appearing between the other dancers getting closer and closer. Melody felt the air leave her lungs, a cold fear clawing up her spine; the other dancers no longer looked happy, their colourful gowns now looking gaudy and harsh. The music's tempo started to increase, and Melody felt herself spinning faster and faster. She could not catch her breath, she was going to pass out; the shadowy figure now loomed closer, his black gloved hand reaching out towards her throat. As the fingers started to squeeze, she felt herself falling, a scream dying on her lips.

Melody awoke, the scream still ringing in her ears, a film of sweat trickled down her cleavage. Looking frantically around, she slowly realised that she was in her bedroom; it had just been a nightmare. Leaning over to switch off her lamp, she glanced at the porcelain doll sitting on the chair by the window; its eyes did seem to look directly at you. Shaking her head at her thoughts, the nightmare had spooked her more than she cared to admit; deciding she would try not to read the journal at bedtime, Melody snuggled down for sleep.

Chapter 3

Early the next morning, after feeding Toby and filling the coffee machine, Melody headed into her craft room. She had an hour to start Lucy's party dress before she would have to head off to the shop. Stopping by her clothes rack of gowns from the trunk, she pulled the rose-pink gown out, lovingly fingering the rosebuds around the neckline. She again felt the pull to try it on; letting go of the gown, it swung back onto the rack as the nightmare played over again in her mind. She had been wearing this gown. Shaking herself mentally, Melody made her way over to the mannequin and the gold gown. Time to start un-picking the seams; the main skirt of the gown would be ample enough material for the two dresses, one for Lucy and another to sell at the shop, with enough left over for a shawl and ribbons. Melody rubbed her hands together in glee; she just loved a project like this.

Walking into the kitchen and pouring herself a coffee, she sat at the kitchen table, her position giving her a direct view into her craft room, which had once been her grandmother's utility room. The light from the large windows bathing it in sunshine made it a perfect room for her crafts; the sink and washing machine, the only remnants of the old room. The skirts of the gown now lay on her craft table, the bodice remained on the mannequin and she was pleased with the progress she had made. Sipping her coffee, she relaxed back, stretching her legs out and rubbing a slumbering Toby with her toe.

Heading back to her craft room, she lifted the fabric up from the table. As she did this, something hard banged against her leg. Lifting the material to look at the underside, Melody noticed an out of place cloth pocket sewn into the lining. "Strange to have a pocket here", she muttered, at the same time reaching into it. Her fingers wrapped around another piece of cloth; she gently pulled the cloth bag out and headed back to the kitchen. Opening the bag, she emptied its contents onto the table. An Emerald and diamond necklace slipped out; as she straightened it out, the filigree gold necklace spread into a fan shape. Melody blinked hard at the main square cut emerald as it shone so brightly, flanked on either side by smaller emeralds and diamonds, the sunshine catching them and bringing them to life with breath-taking sparkles.

"Geez Toby, I think it's real", Melody's voice barely a whisper, Toby's low bark the only other sound in the kitchen. "Oh Tob's, we're late"! Grabbing her tote bag, she hurriedly replaced the necklace into the cloth bag, scooped up the journal, the letters now safely tucked inside its cover and dropped them all into her bag. Grabbing her keys and calling for Toby to follow, she locked up and hurried to her car.

He watched as the girl and her dog got into the car; he had seen her easily swing the trunk into her boot. It looked too light to contain anything anymore, but he was not going to take any chances this time. He was pleased that he had decided to drive around the empty town yesterday. His hunch had paid off, when on spotting her red car pulling out from the private car park at the back of some shops, he had been able to tail her at a safe distance to her home. Watching her drive away from the cluster of cottages, he started the engine. Flicking his cigarette out of the van window, he eased his van onto the road. All he had to do now was discover where she was going, and if the trunk was indeed empty.

As he anticipated, she pulled into the private car park at the back of the shops. Pulling over on the road, he cut the engine as this was a good vantage point to watch her. She pulled the trunk out of the boot, swinging it loosely and headed towards the back of the shop, her dog at her heals. Slipping out of his van and crossing the road, he stood scanning the shops and counted the buildings. He made it the fourth one that she had entered. He quickly headed to the front of the shops and at the fourth one, he stopped and glanced up at the sign, "Simple Crafts" emblazoned above the shop, the window display revealing all types of craft wares.

"Oh Susie, you're a saint", Melody grinned, presenting her shop assistant and friend a freshly made cup of coffee.

Susie laughingly accepted the coffee. "I thought you might be late, I see you had a good time at the boot fair yesterday". Susie nodded towards the back storeroom.

"Oh yes and I have some other bits I brought with me today, a rather nice antique trunk I'm going to use in the new window display, and these silver and enamel peacock scissors", Melody enthused as she reached into her bag and produced the scissors, taking a sip from her coffee lost in thought. Susie shook her head and tutted. When Melody got a window display idea, she was totally absorbed in it till she had it completed.

Abandoning Melody to her window display in progress and heading over to help a customer who was looking at some rather large felted flowers, Susie smiled muttering to herself. "Now if we could just get these sold, it would afford us some much-needed display space".

Taking a step back from the shop, he glanced about noticing a coffee shop on the other side of the road. The iron tables and chairs affording customers a chance to enjoy the early morning sunshine, this would be the perfect place to sit and observe. Making his way over, he sat down at one of the vacant tables and positioning himself to get the best view of the shop, he picked up the shabby dog-eared menu. He pretended to give it a look; soon the waiter appeared and after ordering his coffee, he sat casually watching the trickle of traffic pass by. He could see that the girl was now standing at the window, emptying the display; the trunk sat by the counter.

"Your coffee sir", the waiter placed the coffee on the table, "can I get you anything else"?

"No, that's fine thank you", he replied, willing the waiter to be gone, so he could resume his watch. Adding cream and two heaped sugars to his coffee, he contemplated what he would do next.

The girl disappeared for a moment, reappearing with the trunk. He narrowed his eyes trying to get a better look. She swung the trunk into the window display, lifting the lid. He leaned in closer; it was empty. "Damn", he swore. Leaving some money on the table with his barely touched coffee, he headed back to his van.

Melody stepped back, admiring her latest window display. The trunk propped open and the blue and green silk material pooled out of it in ripples. The peacock feathers angled against the cream felt board at the back, an antique looking sewing box with its lid open, revealing cotton spools and embroidery threads with the peacock scissors balancing against it; balls of yarn and brightly coloured buttons were strategically placed around, which finished the look.

"Stunning", Susie clapped her hands. "You always deliver Mel, this will make customers want to come in and shop".

Melody laughed. Susie was always so positive after a window display was done. "Need anything from the storeroom"? Melody asked picking up the box of old display items.

"We need some yarn and we are low on the baby pink flower buttons. While it's quiet, I'll go get us a pastry, you look hungry", laughing Susie grabbed her purse. They both knew that Susie had a rather sweet tooth and would often use Melody as an excuse to get pastries. Melody made her way to the storeroom, checking on Toby, who was curled up asleep in his bed behind the counter, oblivious to the treats that would soon be arriving. Flicking the lights on and placing the box onto a shelf, she collected the buttons and yarn, humming softly to herself as she headed back out to the shop floor to re-stock the displays.

He pulled his van to a stop two streets away from the girl's cottage. Better to not draw attention by parking nearer. Grabbing his rucksack, he shrugged it onto his back. Pulling his baseball cap low on his head, he made his way on foot, his casual attire of jeans and sweatshirt made him blend in. The eight cottages in the cul-de-sac seemed empty, most of the occupants either away working or running errands. Only two cars parked outside indicated that some neighbours could be home. Slipping through the front gate, he quickly made his way around the side of the cottage, flicking the side gate latch. He looked around, thick hedging on three sides lined the garden, a low fence connecting to the cottage next door that was currently empty. He was sure he couldn't be seen from here, a quick scan of the back revealed all the windows shut tight, noticing two earthenware pots sitting on each side of the backdoor full of red flowers. 'What if', he thought, tipping them carefully, he searched for a key, but no key had been left. Looking back at the old wooden door with its red paint chipping, he decided it wouldn't take much to break it. Taking a look through the door's glass panels, he spied the simple yale lock, and raising his large booted foot, he gave one hard kick, the sound of splintering wood made him still for a moment. Everything remained quiet; no-one had been alerted to his presence. He slowly let his breath out, as he pushed his way inside; the only sound was the door groaning softly.

As soon as Melody pushed the front garden gate open, Toby bounded through, his nose to the ground, a low growl sounding from him as he headed up the path. "Has that cat been here again"? Melody laughed as Toby started to raise his hackles. Misty, the black and white cat who lived two cottages down, had taken to spending the days stretched out on their doorstep sunning herself. She was no-where to be seen at present, always making herself scarce whenever they pulled up, usually just a flash of black heading over the low garden fence that separated her property and Alex's. As she looked over towards Alex's, she noticed his car parked outside. She looked forward to seeing him later, a familiar thrill making her heartbeat faster.

Unlocking the front door, she headed inside, leaving it ajar for Toby, once he had tired of cat hunting. Instantly Melody felt uneasy, the breeze from the front door seemingly too strong. "I know I didn't leave a window open" she mused looking around. Picking up her mail, she headed towards the kitchen; it was as she was entering that she noticed the back door standing wide open, the frame splintered and broken. "Oh god, no", she cried out, looking around the dishevelled kitchen, draws hanging open, chairs overturned. Looking towards her front room, the chaos continued, sofa cushions scattered on the floor, her bureau's draws pulled so far out that they were barely secure on their runners, books and papers scattered everywhere. The sound of Toby barking frantically pulled Melody back from her terror. She had to get them out of here; the burglar could still be here. Turning on her heels, she slammed into a hard chest. As two arms wrapped around her, Melody felt her knees buckle.

"Please", she begged, trying to regain her equilibrium.

"It's okay Mel, it's me Alex", he breathed in her sweet strawberry scented hair as she sagged in relief against him.

"Oh Alex, I've been robbed", Melody gasped, as the tears started to fall freely.

"Wait here, and don't touch anything", Alex instructed, clicking his fingers and signalling for Toby to stay by her. Pulling out his phone and dialling the police, he took the stairs two at a time.

After checking the upstairs and the rest of the cottage, Alex returned, finding Melody perched on the edge of her sofa. "Is it as bad upstairs"?

He nodded. "Once the police give us the all clear, we will need to make a list of what's missing for their report", he spoke softly, pulling Melody to her feet and holding her in his embrace. "It's okay now, Mel, you're safe". She snuggled in closer, the warmth of his body easing the tension she felt, his hands stroking her back as he gently rocked her.

The hours passed in a haze for Melody as Alex dealt with the police, called his business partner Joel to arrange for a new back door to be fitted the next day, and orchestrated the situation. After replacing the splintered wood frame and securing a new lock on the backdoor for the night, Alex felt more at ease. Placing a pen and pad into Melody's hands, Alex gave her an encouraging squeeze. "Time to see what's missing, Mel".

As she trailed from room to room, Melody's frown grew deeper. "I don't understand this Alex, nothing seems to be missing". Her jewellery box still contained all its contents, her laptop sat on the kitchen table. Stopping in the front room, she made her way to the bureau. Looking absently, she tried to remember what she had left in there. Her camera sat in one corner, her iPad and mp3 player beside it; running her hands over the items, she tried to remember. "No way! This doesn't make any sense", she whispered.

Alex leaned in. "What doesn't make sense"?

"The journals, they are gone". Rooting around in the other draws confirmed her suspicions; the journals were missing.

Melody sat at the kitchen table, her mug of coffee warming her icy cold fingers. In the distance, she could hear Alex talking on the phone. Since the police had left, they had put the cottage back to normal, although Melody felt it would never feel normal again.

"I think Toby deserves an extra biscuit", Alex announced as he reached for Toby's treat tin. "What a good boy Tob's alerting me", he praised as Toby inhaled his biscuit and looked eagerly for another. "Although I still think that we need to install an alarm, I've arranged for our best security alarm to be fitted first thing tomorrow". Melody silently nodded her head. If it had not been for Toby's frantic barking alerting Alex, she did not know how long she would have stood there in shock. Alex had always wanted her to get an alarm; he had every security detail covered in his own home. She had often teased him, wondering if he had the crown jewels hidden away inside to protect.

"Oh my god", Melody's voice barely a whisper, had Alex instantly concerned, as she shakily rose from the table and headed over to the front room.

He was by her side. "What is it, Mel", he gently placed his hand on her waist.

"I forgot all about this", she gestured, pulling a cloth bag from her tote bag. "I found it this morning in a secret lining pocket in a gown I was unpicking". Tipping the contents into Alex's hand, the necklace sparkled brightly. "It's from the same trunk the journals were in. Was this what the thief was looking for"?

Pulling Melody down onto the sofa with him, Alex examined the necklace. He had had a lot of experience with expensive items his customers needed securing, it was without a doubt that this was real and most definitely worth a fortune; his gut instinct was never wrong.

"I think it was exactly what the thief was looking for, but why did he think you had it"? Alex growled, wanting to punch the thief for scaring Melody. "We should put this away in my safe for the time being until we figure out what to do" he sighed, looking at Melody as she nodded her approval. "I won't be long. Lock the door behind me and keep Toby with you" he said as he made his way back to his cottage. As he scanned the surrounding area, his anger grew. No one would frighten Melody again; his sudden aggression and overly protective response left him feeling shocked to his core.

Standing at the sink, rinsing the coffee cups, Melody's mind wandered over the evening's events. Why had the thief taken the journals? What was the necklace doing hidden in the gown? Who could have known she had the trunk? Unanswered questions swirled about in her head. A knock on the back door signalled Alex's return; hurrying over to let him in, she eyed his holdall clasped in his hand. Alex grinned sheepishly.

"Hope you don't mind, I thought I'd bring my overnight things. I didn't think you'd want to be alone tonight".

"Alex I…", Melody bit her lip to stop it from wobbling, a riot of expressions crossing her face.

"It's okay Mel, I just mean I'll stay on the sofa, you'll sleep better knowing I'm here". Melody's relief was evident on her face.

"I can fix the bed in my grandmother's old room for you Alex", she smiled, half expecting him to tease her.

"No, the sofa's fine, just a pillow and blanket will do for me". He stifled a yawn as he headed into the front room and put his holdall down.

"It's been a long day", Melody sighed as she returned to the front room placing the blanket and pillow onto the sofa, a contented sigh escaping her lips as Alex wrapped his arms around her, the feeling of his warm body pressed into her back.

"It sure has", Alex muttered against her hair, trailing feather light kisses down her neck. Melody spun around in his arms and leaned in closer. Rising onto her toes, she captured his lips with hers, kissing him and then nipping at his bottom lip. Growling, Alex scooped her up and kissed her deeply. She groaned as she felt herself melting into him, all that existed was this moment. "Enough little minx", Alex's strained voice jerked her back to reality. Pulling back, she looked into his eyes, now dark blue pools of barely contained desire. "Off to bed with you right now, if you know what's good for you", he reached out and caressed her face.

Turning her face into his palm, she placed a kiss and whispered. "Goodnight Alex", stepping back she turned and headed for the stairs.

As he watched her head off to bed, Alex smiled to himself. It was good he had decided to stay; she would sleep better knowing he was here and he would too knowing that she was safe. Calling a halt to their kissing had been the hardest thing he'd had to do, but she was too vulnerable after all that had happened tonight. He couldn't forgive himself if she had regretted being with him in the morning. He reached into his holdall and retrieved his gun, slipping it under his pillow. He settled down, his thoughts turning to Joel. He would feel better once his friend arrived in the morning and they could secure the cottage. Joel had been a good friend for years now. Having always had each other's back whilst serving in the air-force, the pair had formed a close bond; they regarded each other more like brothers now. After they had left the air-force, it had been rough for them trying to find a place in the world. All the military drilling leaving them feeling at a loss being civilians again, Joel's idea to start their own security firm had been their saving grace; without this he was sure they would have drifted along in life without a purpose. He would be forever grateful for his friend's savvy business sense and drive. Even when his wife had died, and Alex could only find solace at the bottom of a whisky bottle, Joel had been there dragging him out of his stupor, forcing him to live life again, even re-locating their planned second security business to the local town where Alex had announced he was moving to and temporarily setting himself up there to help get it up and running. Alex rubbed at his eyes, his memories of the past flicking through his mind. He lay still, listening to the sounds of the cottage settling down. Pulling the blanket up, he slowly drifted off into a light sleep.

Chapter 4

The smell of bacon and coffee stirred Melody from her sleep. With the thoughts of the previous day flooding her mind, she quickly showered, deciding on jeans and a watermelon pink t-shirt. Melody quickly dressed, pulling a brush through her hair, she left it down. Stuffing her feet into her trainers, Melody went to investigate the yummy aromas heading from the kitchen. "Morning, beautiful", Alex called out from the front room.

She turned to look at him. "Morning, Alex". He was showered and dressed, his hair still damp, his face freshly shaved.

"Your breakfast's keeping warm in the grill, and there's fresh coffee too", he grinned. "Joel will be here soon, so I thought I'd better make a start. I fed Toby the leftover Chinese food from last night, he seemed ravenous".

"He always is", Melody laughed, taking her breakfast to the table. Toby strolled over and plopped down at her feet, doing his best to look like a starving stray dog.

Pouring them both a coffee, Alex sat down at the table. "So what's the plan today, Mel? Will you be going into work"?

Nibbling on a bit of toast, Melody shrugged her shoulders. "I was supposed to be, but I can't leave with the house being fitted with the new back door and the alarm system".

Alex leaned in "Leave it to me Mel, I'll oversee the work. You head into the shop, the change of scene will do you good".

Melody smiled. He really was great, "Oh, that's brilliant Alex, you're the best". His warm smile reaching his eyes had her toes curling in her trainers. Blushing to her roots, she leant down and dropped a bit of bacon for Toby.

Joel arrived as Melody was leaving. She waved at him as she pulled away, recognising his dark blue van, the Knight and Brooks Security signage slashing down the side. He tooted his horn in response. Alex appeared at the door, rushing down to help Joel offload the new backdoor from the van.

"Hey Alex, we'll get this offloaded first, then I want to hear all about this break in business last night". Joel motioned towards the backdoors of the van. After hefting the new door and all the security equipment into the back garden, Alex poured them both a coffee and filled him in on the troubling theft. "I have a feeling this particular thief will be back", Joel said scratching his head.

"Exactly my thoughts", Alex agreed, "but I'm not going to make it easy for the bugger", he growled, scanning the garden as if expecting to see the thief pop up from behind a bush.

"Have you informed the police about the necklace yet"?

Alex shifted his weight uneasily. "Not yet Joel, we are still uncertain what we are going to do. I feel that once we hand it over to them, we will lose some of the control over the thief". Joel stared hard at Alex; he was always doing things his way. Never once had he doubted his gut. He just hoped he was right this time.

"So what's our next move"? Alex grinned. He knew that Joel would back him up on this.

"Well, let's get started securing this place first and then I have a few ideas". Picking up his tools, they started to work.

Arriving at the shop, armed with cinnamon buns and coffee, Melody made her way to the counter, after settling Toby in his bed with a rawhide chew and his favourite ball. She busily set about the shop, checking stock and straightening displays. When she was satisfied, she flipped the open sign on the door and after unlocking it, headed to her seat behind the counter. Susie would be here soon. She was looking forward to seeing her. Sipping her coffee, Melody booted up the computer; she opened the search engine, trying several searches on old trunks, emerald necklaces leather bound journals and coming up empty.

She sat back, reaching into her bag, she pulled out the journal. The letters tucked inside the front cover falling out, she picked them up and sliding the red ribbon off, she unfolded the one with no envelope, its sweeping bold script penned across the page.

June 7th 1952

My dearest Christina,

I do not dare to attend your party this night for fear this would be frowned upon. However, I really cannot resist seeing you again. My only request is for you to slip away from the

*party at 8 pm and unlock the French doors in the library,
where I will then slip inside and meet you. It will be our secret
rendezvous. I have something I need to tell you.*

Forever yours
Jack

Melody gazed at the letter. "Who are you Christina"? A
sudden idea formed; quickly, she stabbed at the keys on
the keyboard, typing "Christina Elizabeth Trafford" and hit
search. Scrolling through the results, one caught her eye; it
was a story in an old newspaper archive. The headline was
dated 18th June 1952.

*LEFT FOR DEAD LADY CHRISTINA TRAFFORD
AND THE MISSING HEIRLOOM*

*Police are still baffled as to who assaulted Lord Edward
and Lady Elise Trafford's daughter, leaving her for dead on
the night of her eighteenth birthday party and escaping with
her priceless heirloom emerald necklace. While every effort to
track down the perpetrator continues, police seem no closer to
solving this crime. Police inspector Collins would only comment. "At this time, we have one or two suspects". He would
not be drawn to offer any more on the case stating, "As this is
an ongoing investigation, it is not possible to reveal any further
details".*

Melody turned off the computer, her mind reeling. This
had to be the necklace she had found that was now securely
placed in Alex's safe, but how did it end up in the gown?
The chimes above the door tinkled, rousing Melody from

her thoughts. "Good morning", Melody greeted the two customers entering the store. The two ladies' bright hellos rang out clearly, as they headed in different directions to browse around the shop.

Susie bustled into the shop, her cheerful hello making Melody look up from her paperwork. "Oh dear, Mel you look exhausted", Susie grimaced seeing the dark smudges beneath Melody's eyes. Passing Susie a coffee, Melody filled her in on the break in. "You poor thing, at least you had Alex and Toby with you", she smiled, devouring the cinnamon bun and throwing Toby a large crumb.

"He really is an angel, he stayed to oversee the new backdoor being fitted, and the security alarm installation", Melody enthused, feeling an overwhelming need to call him and check how things were going.

"Do I detect a little romance, Mel"? Susie teased, knowing full well that they had been dancing around one another for months.

Melody sighed contentedly, the thoughts of Alex holding her and kissing her still fresh in her mind. "We um, well, I guess yes. We have kissed and it was so good", she absentmindedly touched her lips as if his kiss had left a mark. "We have decided to take it slow. Neither of us wants to mess this up; our friendship is too important to rush things. Besides, he knows I've been hurt before, but oh Susie, he's just so amazing, not to mention drop dead gorgeous". Blushing, Melody jumped up from her seat. "Come on Tob's, time for you to stretch your legs". Picking up his ball, Melody headed to the storeroom and out the back to the car park.

Susie knew when to leave well alone, not probing any further. After all, she knew that for Melody, it was a fragile thing, a new relationship. She was pleased they were finally getting together. He, she was sure was good for her. Melody's last boyfriend Zack had left Melody disillusioned and empty. He had always tried to control Melody and when finally she put her foot down, refusing to cancel her invitation to spend a long planned weekend with her two best friends instead of staying at home with him, which she knew was just another way to exert his control, his true colours had finally revealed themselves. He had petulantly given her an ultimatum that either she chooses him over her friends, or he would leave her for good. Fortunately, she had chosen her friends and she was glad Melody had finally seen through his games and realised she was better off without him. Smiling contentedly to herself, Susie cleared away the coffee cups. "Yes, Alex's a good one and Melody deserves a good man", she muttered to herself.

As he sat waiting in the reception of the care home, the smell of disinfectant and warm cooked vegetables assailed him. The threadbare rug looked old and worn as did the assortment of chairs placed around the small area, a table with a collection of reading materials the only other furniture in the room. This was not the care home he would have chosen for his father, but it was all he could afford at present and for how long he would be able to stay here, he could not guarantee. The money his father had stored up was nearly all gone; soon he would fix all this, he vowed to himself, but for now this place would just have to do. Looking down at his scuffed boots and tatty jeans, he shifted uneasily. Yes, one day he would be wearing the best designer clothes and place his father in the best care home money could buy, he would show them all! Absent-mindedly, he rubbed his rucksack, his eyes narrowing in distaste. He truly felt the common staff were beneath him, if only they knew of his upper-class heritage than his present circumstances portrayed.

Haughtily tilting his chin, he watched as Craig, one of the home's carers approached. "Hello Timothy, your dad is all ready to see you now; he's in the dayroom as usual", gesturing for him to follow. Timothy grabbed his rucksack tighter and followed Craig into the dayroom. At the farthest end of the room, sitting by the tall windows, he spotted his father, his frail stooped frame dwarfed in a high back chair, his head bowed, a coverlet over his knees and his cane resting against the arm of the chair, the lion head handle glinting menacingly in the sunlight. How many times had he felt that cane strike him as his father meted out punishments, he had lost count. "He's not too good today I'm afraid. I'm not sure he will recognise you", Craig spoke softly, jerking him from his troubled thoughts.

"Thank you Craig", Timothy said curtly, all but dismissing him. Craig turned to leave, heading over to another resident, all the while repeating his calming mantra under his breath; he would not let that jumped up little prick get to him again.

Bracing himself mentally, Timothy made his way over and sat opposite his father. "Hello father".

The old man lifted his head. "Timothy", his father croaked.

Leaning in, he took his father's hands in his. "Yes father, it's me and I have great news! I have the journals", he motioned to his rucksack. "It won't be long now father, I'm sure they will reveal where it is". Pulling the journals from his rucksack, he placed them into his father's hands. He felt his pleasure grow as he watched his father's interest deepen while he studied them; finally he would be proud of him.

Philip's cold green eyes settled on his son. Thrusting the journals roughly back into Timothy's hands, he snarled. "Where's the other one? You are missing one boy, the first one was started in 1952. These two are 1953 and 1954, you incompetent fool", his sharp accusing voice momentarily rendered Timothy back to his adolescent years.

"But father are you s-sure"? He stammered. "I searched everywhere, it was the last trunk and she only had two…". Timothy fell silent, his father's disappointment cutting him deep.

"Well, who are you young man? Do you have my dinner"? His father commanded, rapping his cane on Timothy's chair. Startled, he looked up, his father's eyes, clouded and confused, now looking pathetic and old, all traces of his anger now gone.

Knowing he would not get any more sense from his father now, Timothy rose from his seat. "Goodbye father, see you next week", he muttered under his breath. Shoving the journals into his rucksack, he made his way out of the care home to his van, scowling at anyone that crossed his path. "I'll show him", he muttered angrily to himself, his thoughts turning back to the journals in his rucksack. They may still hold the key, hopefully. Before his next visit to his father, he would have read them. "I can't risk not having the missing one, just in case", he mused, swearing repeatedly. "Three bloody journals!"

Susie insisted that Melody should head off early from work and after insisting several times that she would be fine to lock up, she shooed Melody off to her car. After a quick call to Alex to check on the progress at home, she reluctantly started the car. With the radio playing, she sang along to Carly Rae Jepson's, "Call me maybe". Her mood lifted as she thought of Alex; she was definitely under his spell, she thought with a grin as she sung the words. With the sun shining, Melody drove through the busy town; Toby's head hanging outside of the car window, the breeze lifting his ears and making passers-by smile and point.

Melody turned into Sarah's street; she hadn't planned to visit her today but found the familiar route too tempting to avoid. The cherry blossom trees lining the pathways in full bloom always made her feel happy, the large houses set back from the road each boasting a magnificent immaculate flowerbed display and highly manicured lawns. Melody always imagined the occupants on their hands and knees on the lawn, measuring the blades of grass to get just the right length. She laughed as she imagined the shock on their faces if they ever saw her wild cottage garden, so totally disorganised with Toby's toys scattered about the lawn. Biting down another fit of laughter, Melody pulled onto the drive, parking neatly behind Sarah's 4x4 range rover. Pushing open the front door, Melody tutted to herself. "This is not very security conscious, sis", she would have this to tease her about for quite a while to come. Stepping into the kitchen, the smell of warm cookies instantly greeted her.

"Aunty Mel, we're making cookies", an excited Lucy squealed, waving her spatula in the air.

"Mmm, smells good sweetie", Melody laughed, placing a kiss on top of Lucy's soft blonde head. For once, Toby ignored the smells of food and bounded over to greet Rex, Sarah's beagle, as they began their greeting rituals. Melody walked over and opened the patio doors, shooing them into the garden. "Go play outside, you two silly things", she laughed, shutting the doors as Toby and Rex excitedly bounded around the lawn, tails wagging.

"Coffee, love"? Sarah appeared from the pantry, wiggling a mug at Melody. Looking at her sister, she smiled; they looked so different from each other. While Melody was fair like her mum, Sarah was the image of their dad with his dark brooding looks. A lump caught in her throat as she still missed her parents terribly. The car crash that had stolen them from their lives four years ago still seemed so unreal; watching Sarah across the kitchen, her dark hair piled on top of her head in a messy bun, a smudge of flour on her nose and apron around her waist, her warm chocolate brown eyes turned darker when she was worried or upset. She was slightly shorter than Melody; the three inch difference in height a constant bone of contention, with Sarah teasing that Melody stole all the height genes leaving Sarah born a year later with less. At five foot three, her fuller figure gave her a cuddly approachable vibe.

"Oh yes please", she smiled, pulling herself from her reverie as she stole a cookie from the plate on the kitchen island.

"So Mel, how's things with you, you look tired"? Sarah asked, frowning as she placed Melody's coffee down in front of her, glancing warily across at Lucy.

Melody shook her head. "I'm fine, sis".

Picking up the silent entreaty, Sarah took the hint. "Lucy, why don't you go watch some television, your favourite show will be starting soon".

"Okay mummy. Can I take a cookie", she pleaded hopping up and down.

"Just one, love", Sarah smiled as Lucy grabbed the biggest one and headed out of the kitchen, grabbing her doll from the chair as she went.

Taking a seat at the opposite side of the kitchen island, Sarah leaned forward on her elbows, fixing her gaze on Melody. "Now Mel, spill". Melody knew this conversation was not going to be easy, but after spending the last twenty minutes telling her all the details of the break-in, she had not expected Sarah's reaction to be quite this intense. "What do you mean, no! Of course you must come and stay"! Sarah exclaimed, wringing the t-towel in exasperation.

"It's fine sis, as I said Alex's fitted a new sturdy back door with a deadbolt lock and a safety chain, and even as we speak, he and Joel are installing the best security alarm their company provides". Gazing down at her hands, blushing, she added, "He even insists on staying over till I'm feeling comfortable again".

Pouring them both another coffee, Sarah chewed her bottom lip. "Well, I don't like the thought of you on your own, but knowing Alex's there looking after you, I guess I can take some comfort in that; but promise me you'll come stay with us if you feel the need".

Feeling that she had got off lightly, Melody nodded her head in acceptance, adding, "Now let's talk about something more cheerful. Lucy's party dress is coming along quite nicely". The change of subject had had the desired effect.

Melody spent the next hour chatting with Sarah about the dress and party plans, the only tell-tale sign of her sister's anguish over the break-in showing in the overly tight hug she gave her as she headed out to the car.

"Promise, you'll call me if you need anything", Sarah emphasised the last word.

"I will, I promise", Melody sighed, bending down to kiss Lucy goodbye, placing a kiss on her sister's cheek, she turned and making her way to the car, she called to Toby. "Come on boy, let's go".

The sound of laughter from the kitchen made Melody quicken her step down the hall, the pizza boxes and bag of groceries in her arms holding no interest for Toby as he scooted past her into the kitchen to greet their guests. Finding Alex and Joel lounging at the kitchen table, their legs stretched out, Melody stole a look at them. Joel was as tall as Alex at six foot three; his dark black hair still cut in an army style with short back and sides and longer on the top, which suited him well. Wearing khaki coloured t-shirt and cargo pants, he looked ready for action; his well-defined muscles slightly smaller than Alex's. Flicking her eyes towards Alex, she devoured the sight of him, his white t-shirt stretched over his pecs, strong arms resting on his legs and his biceps bulging. Meeting his eyes, Melody blushed as she saw the amusement dancing in them, realising she had been caught staring. She abruptly placed the grocery bag and pizza boxes onto the table.

"I thought you two might be hungry; I picked up a couple of pizzas", she explained, pointing at the pizza boxes, then reaching into the grocery bag, she pulled out some bottled beer. "I got some chilled beer for you too, thought you might be thirsty".

Joel laughingly took the beer. "Oh Mel, just what we needed, you're a star". After collecting some plates and a bottle opener, Melody pulled a chair out next to Alex and sat down. "You sure know the way to a man's heart, pizza and beer", Joel laughed opening the beers and handing one to Melody.

Grabbing a slice of pizza and offering it to Melody, Alex leaned closer. "So how has your day been, Mel"?

Biting into the offered pizza, she looked between Alex and Joel. "Well, I learned something very interesting about the necklace".

Alex and Joel leaned in closer, their faces both registering their keen interest. "Go on", Joel prompted, as she hesitated.

"Well, as the journals belonged to Christina Trafford, I decided to do a search on google for her. Turns out that on her eighteenth birthday party, she was attacked and the heirloom emerald necklace she had been wearing was stolen. The newspaper article described it and it's just like the one I found". Stopping abruptly, she looked uncertainly at Alex.

As if sensing her unspoken question, he reached out and took her hand. "I've told him all about it", he said, nodding towards Joel. Sighing in relief, Melody continued filling them in on all she had learned, watching as Alex and Joel sat silently listening, occasionally glancing at one another, a worried frown settling on Alex's face.

"I'd say, we have to tread really carefully here", Joel announced after Melody came to the end of her story.

"Yes I agree, and I'm thinking of making some discreet enquiries about this Christina for our next move", Alex spoke softly, directing his glance at Melody, waiting for her approval.

"Yes I agree, and if we could find out if she is still alive, we could visit her, maybe even reunite her with the necklace"? Alex and Joel nodded their approval.

"But from now on Mel, you need to keep an eye out for anything unusual, or that seems out of place. You have to be extra careful".

Alex's serious voice held Melody's attention; forcing down her mouthful of pizza, feeling herself tensing as nervousness coursed through her, she croaked out.

"Okay, I will". Taking a gulp of beer, she cleared her throat. "I still have a journal; I took it with me to the shop the day of the break-in". Reaching into her bag, she withdrew it and placed it on the table. "It starts a few days after the attack on Christina. She says she lost her memory, but from what I have read so far, I'm sure the gown I'm unpicking and found the necklace inside, is the same one she was wearing the night of her party and attack".

"My god", Joel exclaimed, slamming his fist on the table.

Raising an eyebrow at him, Alex motioned for him to go on. "I think that blasted thief is after the journals for clues to find the missing necklace. Let's just hope he doesn't know there are three, or else…". Alex's frown and the slight shake of his head, silencing him. Turning back to Melody, he noticed her eyes nervously darting around the room.

Alex reached out and firmly clasped her hands in his. "It's good that we have the security alarm installed now", he soothed, loosening his grip and rubbing her hands gently, smiling encouragingly. He apprised Melody of all the security measures they had installed, releasing her hands to slide a piece of paper across the table towards her. He nodded towards it. "The security codes, Mel, best if you can memorise them".

"Yes and then destroy all evidence", Joel laughed, winking at her in mock conspiracy, taking Alex's lead and trying to lighten the mood as he tucked into another slice of pizza.

Alex glared at Joel. "I think it best she doesn't want to leave it lying around. It's important to put it somewhere safe or dispose of it", he insisted, raising his hands in defeat. Joel looked at Melody, her head bent as she nervously chewed on her pizza. He could tell that Alex was in full protect mode, and could see why his friend had fallen so hard for her. She was quite beautiful, her blonde curls catching the sunlight, making her look like an angel as it fell softly around her shoulders, her slender figure and well-endowed curves would get any man wanting to protect her. He was glad that Alex had found her. She was just what he needed and by the looks of it, she was happily besotted with Alex. He felt happier, knowing when he eventually headed back to the city, he wouldn't be leaving Alex alone.

"Do you have much left to do"? Melody queried, bringing Joel back from his musings.

"Just a couple of tests on the alarm, then clearing up the mess in the garden", he grinned, looking at all the woodchips and tools lying scattered by the open backdoor.

"I want to put a safety chain on the front door", Alex chimed in, "shouldn't take me too long". Throwing a pizza crust at an eager Toby, Alex walked over to the sink to rinse his hands.

"That's great! I'm going to disappear in my craft room for a while, to continue working on Lucy's party dress. You know where I am if you need anything", Melody smiled, reaching Alex's side, she passed him a towel.

Placing a finger under her chin and lifting her face up to look into her eyes, the gold flecks more pronounced as he kissed the tip of her nose, he said, "I thought we could take Toby for a walk later, Mel, if you fancy"?

Wrapping her arms around his hips, she leaned in and kissed his lips. "Mm, sounds good", she whispered.

Clearing his throat, Joel loudly announced. "Well, I'd better get back to work. This mess won't clean itself up". Winking at them both, he headed off, singing an out of tune song.

After seeing Joel off and insisting that he drop by for dinner with them soon, Melody left Alex waving goodbye and went inside to find Toby's lead. "Well, Joel sure seemed happy", Alex's softly spoken words felt like a caress as he nuzzled her neck.

"He did", Melody agreed turning around into Alex's arms, "has he got any plans for the evening"?

"He's taking his latest date out to the movies", his voice was husky, as he trailed hot kisses down her neck.

"Mm, that's nice".

"The kisses or the movies"? he enquired, laughing softly. He pulled back to look at her. Running a finger along his unshaven jaw and then tracing his lips, she looked into his now intense grey-blue eyes. Capturing her finger in his mouth, Alex pulled her tighter to him.

"Oh, the movies of course", Melody teased, placing her hands around his neck, her fingers spearing into his thick hair, pulling him down to capture his lips.

An over excited Toby, having spied his lead on the chair, started barking repeatedly, breaking the spell. "I guess he wants his walk", Melody murmured, reluctantly pulling out of Alex's arms. Suppressing a sigh, Alex grabbed their jackets and after securing a bouncing Toby, Alex showed her how to set the alarm. It felt good to know the cottage would be safer from now on.

Melody settled into bed reflecting on the evening she had spent with Alex. Even with the alarm set, it was reassuring to know he was just below her bedroom in the front room. He had made her laugh with stories of his and Joel's antics on different jobs they had done and the light feeling had been a blessed relief, until she had brought up the break-in and the mood had then turned serious.

Alex's cryptic, "We are working on a plan", was all he would say on the matter. Try as she might, he would not be drawn on the subject further, instead distracting her with kisses and she admitted to herself she was quite happy to let the matter go.

Chapter 5

Alex arrived at work early the next day. His first call to Frank, the local cop, had him feeling more settled. He had always found Frank helpful when dealing with him on various security contracts; the fact that he had agreed to look into the Trafford's off the book was an encouraging start, the more information they had the sounder their plan would be. His next call to Joe at the local newspaper had ended in a decision to meet at one at mama's pizza place, which gave him a few hours to sort through some paper-work and chase up some unpaid bills.

Having poured himself a coffee, he paused at Jane's desk; his ever efficient receptionist had left the file he had requested in the middle of her desk. Looking at her neat pile of folders in her inbox, he smiled to himself. She was one of the best assets of this business, always punctual and eager to learn, staying on late without grumbling if a particular case needed additional attention, speaking her mind if she felt something needed to be rectified or needed a different perspective. Pulling her photo frame around, Alex looked at it. Her smiling eyes as she gazed adoringly at her husband Karl and their twin boys, a moment captured forever, he mused. Her red hair cropped short, the same colour as her boys, the freckles on the boys' flushed faces bringing his thoughts to Melody. Would their children have adorable freckles too? Catching his thoughts, "Slow down Alex", he admonished himself, as he moved the photo back into its original position.

Grabbing the folder, he headed to his desk, looking at the logo, a single rose with the words, "Hopes & Dreams" scrolled across the middle. Flipping the folder open, he looked at the list of names of his best men he had appointed to the security detail. The layout of the esteemed Crafton hotel spread before him, he looked over it again. It had been checked and double checked, the large ballroom exits marked out for security, the highly anticipated event in just over two weeks would be attended by all the top businesses and well to do elite; even a few celebrities had confirmed their support.

The charity event would be successful, he knew as he looked at the invitation in bold gold script against the black card. He read, 'Crafton hotel presents the Hopes & Dreams charity gala', the date and time inserted beneath and boasting a list of entertainment and a three-course meal with champagne, after which was a live auction with a speech on the charity's cancer work to end the evening. Sitting back, he fingered the invitation where his name was inserted and a plus one. They had decided that he was going to be attending this event undercover as a guest; the price of the ticket had been covered by the hotel as part of the contract and with Joel happily taking the lead on this job, he would just be there to make sure everything ran smoothly. He had to get a move on and ask Melody to be his plus one. No doubt she would want time to buy a dress and organise all the things girls liked to do for these things; he just hoped she would agree.

Joel and Jane's cheerful call of good morning pulled him from his reverie. Shuffling the papers back into the folder and placing the invite into his jacket pocket, he called out, "I'm in my office Joel, morning Jane".

Joel appeared at his door. "Hey Alex, you been here long"?

Glancing at the clock, he grimaced. "Yes and the men will be here soon for their assignments". Indicating for Joel to sit down, he leaned forward. "Before they arrive, I want to run an idea pass you. I haven't worked out all the kinks but I think I've got a way of flushing Melody's thief out". Clicking the intercom, Alex instructed, "Hold all my calls, Jane and can you bring in two coffees, please".

"Yes boss", Jane's playful voice boomed back.

Joel looked across the desk at Alex, his expression suddenly serious. He leaned in, "so what's the plan"?

Pulling the brush through her hair, Melody looked at her reflection, her golden curls bouncing back as she eased the brush through them. Winding the front of her hair into coils, she secured it back off her face with a butterfly comb, its wings studded with tiny red gems catching the light. After applying a light coat of mascara and a little red lipstick, she sat back in satisfaction. Glancing at her deep red silk blouse and black pencil skirt, she decided she would pass muster for an evening with her friends. Slipping from the stool, she grabbed her black peep toe shoes and bag. A glance at her watch made her quicken her pace down the stairs. Checking Toby had everything he needed for the evening and slipping on her shoes, she set the alarm and made for her car.

Pulling her car into the busy car park, Melody glanced at the welcoming sight of the restaurant's familiar entrance. On either side of the doors stood double ball topiaries twinned with fairy lights, the dark interior aglow with subdued lighting, and the smell of good food permeating the air. Walking in, she spotted her friends, Lindsey and Charlotte already waiting for her at the bar. They turned and waved as she headed over to them.

"We got you a drink, Mel", Charlotte smiled handing her a glass of white wine.

"So tell us all", Lindsey gushed, as she reached in to hug her.

"Yes, have you and hunky Alex finally got together", Charlotte chimed in, wiggling her eyebrows at her. Sipping her wine, Melody looked at her two friends. Lindsey, a bubbly slim brunette, with soft blue eyes and a killer smile was only a year younger than Melody but looked slightly older with her hair pulled back in a tight chignon; she was dressed in a navy pinstriped trouser suit and had obviously come straight from the solicitor's office where she worked as a legal secretary.

Melody had entered the solicitor's firm that particular morning months ago, feeling lost and nervous for an appointment to deal with her grandmother's will. Lindsey had seemed to read her well and had put her at ease, lighting the mood with her quick wit and sense of humour and they had soon become fast friends.

Charlotte had been friends with Melody for years, catching up every time she visited her grandmother. Her short blonde hair worn in spikes, the ends were coloured pink today, her mischievous grey eyes never missing a thing.

"Well", they said in unison, pulling Melody back to reality.

"We have", Melody grinned as her two friends whooped and punched the air. Filling them in on the details, Melody felt again how lucky she was to have them in her life.

"On a different note, we have a new receptionist at the vets', Karl", Charlotte whispered dramatically, "and he's dreamy".

"He better watch out", Lindsey laughed, rolling her eyes. "Didn't you have a thing for the locum vet last month", she gulped out between laughter.

"Oh yes, but he's moved on now and this one's much nicer", she laughed back. Working at the vets' as a veterinary nurse for the past year, Charlotte was always on the lookout for any single men that graced their door. Her motto was, if they had a pet, they surely had to be stable.

"God help us", Lindsey laughed, winking at Melody, as they all fell into fits of giggles.

A discreet cough had them all glancing up at the waiter hovering by them. "Your table is ready, ladies". Gesturing towards the dining area, the waiter led them across and after seating them, handed out the menus. "I'm Guy, your waiter for this evening. Can I get you more drinks", he offered, standing with his pen poised to take their order.

"Oh yes, three white wines, please", Melody asked, smiling up at him.

"And I'll have the chicken salad", Lindsey chimed in.

"Dieting again", Charlotte teased, licking her lips and adding, "I'll have the fish and chips".

"Make that two fish and chips", Melody spoke, throwing a guilty look at Lindsey as the waiter nodded and headed off to get their order.

As he made his way over to the ladies table carrying the tray of wine, Guy noticed in the far corner, a man sitting staring at the ladies, his limp hair and sallow cheeks giving him an uncared-for look, a sneer on his face. If there was going to be trouble tonight, Guy was sure this man was it. Placing the wine on the table and catching an appreciative stare from the one they called Charlotte, he smiled. She was pretty, her pink dipped spikes and mischievous eyes holding him captive. Shaking his head to clear his thoughts, he turned to leave, deciding it would be best to go and see if he could take the creepy man's order and check the situation out. He didn't want any trouble here tonight; looking again towards the corner where the man was sitting, he saw that the table was now empty, he had gone. "Well that sorts that", he mumbled in relief, heading over to collect the menus to take to the next table of waiting guests.

"You're incorrigible", Lindsey admonished Charlotte, wiggling her finger at her flirtatious friend.

"Oh Lind's, it's only a bit of fun", she grinned back. "We can't all be serious like you, have you even made a move on Andy"? Blushing, Lindsey thought of Andy, a junior solicitor at her firm; she had had a crush on him since she had started there and had confided this to her two friends. He didn't even seem to see her as a woman, always brisk and work orientated whenever she was around.

"Don't start that again", she warned, frowning at Charlotte.

Sensing the hurt in her friend's voice, Melody quickly changed the subject. "I forgot to mention something girls". Taking a furtive look around and lowering her voice, she continued. "I was burgled the other day". They turned towards her, both shocked by her announcement.

"You what"! Lindsey gasped while Charlotte sat open mouthed.

"Well, I didn't really have anything stolen, just a couple of journals", she shrugged, "guess it could have been worse". Filling them in on the events, stopping every now and then to double check that no-one was listening, she explained how she had discovered the necklace, and whom she thought it belonged to, the fact that Alex had now got the necklace safely tucked away, she sat back and took a large sip of her wine.

"Trafford's", Lindsey whispered frowning, "I'm sure our firm has a file on them, quite a well to do family, we handled their estate sale".

Melody leaned forward eagerly. "Could you look to see if there is an address on the file, Lind's? I've been thinking about trying to meet Christina, if she's still alive".

Looking into Melody's worried eyes, Lindsey felt herself bristle. "I'll try Mel, but if I do, you can't let on it was me who provided the address, it's probably breaking all the rules".

"I promise, Lind's", Melody's sincere face alleviating some of the worry.

Promising to call Melody the next day and saying their goodbyes, Lindsey headed to her car, noticing the man behind the wheel of the white van parked next to her. She shivered, his eyes seeming to follow her every move. "Pull yourself together, Lind's", she muttered, all this talk of break-ins and accessing confidential files really had gotten to her. If she wasn't careful, she would start seeing monsters lurking in the shadows.

Driving home that evening, Melody could not wait to see Alex and fill him in on her news. It was a stroke of luck that Lindsey was willing to look at the file and maybe provide them with an address. If Christina was still alive, she would arrange to visit her first and get a feel of the situation before reuniting the necklace and journal with their rightful owner. Glancing in her rear-view mirror, Melody frowned. The same white van was still behind her; she had noticed it when pulling out of the restaurant car park. Shrugging off her suspicions, she sighed. She was letting the break-in get to her again and decided she was just reacting to having talked about it to her friends this evening. Turning into her cul-de-sac, she took a furtive glance once again into her mirror. The van had slowed but wasn't indicating to follow her turn. Parking her car, she was relieved to see the cottage's lights burning brightly; Alex was inside. Opening her front door, she threw a last glance over her shoulder; the van was stationary, parked just outside her turning, its lights off. A prickle of fear gripped her. "Alex", she yelled in fear, turning back to the door. Toby and Alex appeared in lightning speed.

"Melody, is everything okay"? He asked, concern etched on his face.

"I think I was followed", she gulped, pointing towards the road as Alex rushed past her looking at the road, his hands fisted at his sides. Following him, Melody frowned. "It's gone, the van, it's gone", her voice barely a whisper.

Taking Melody into the house and sitting her at the kitchen table, he squatted down in front of her. "You're as white as a sheet". He took her hands in his; they were as cold as ice, her eyes wide with fright. "When did you think you were being followed"?

"I noticed the van when I pulled out of the r-restau-rant", she stuttered "I just got spooked, I think. I'm just over-reacting", she muttered, her smile wavering and tears filling her eyes.

"No Mel, you were right to be suspicious; it's better to be cautious. We still don't know who we are dealing with". Standing, he headed to the kitchen cupboard, returning with a tumbler of brandy. "Here, drink this", his voice gruff, as he handed her the drink. The brandy burned as it went down her throat making Melody blink rapidly as her tears threatened to spill down her face. Plucking the glass from her fingers and placing it on the table, Alex pulled her to her feet and into his arms. Stroking her head, he gently soothed her. "You're safe, Mel. It's okay, I've got you baby". Resting her head against his chest, she felt the tension ease as the brandy warmed her insides and leaning in closer to Alex, the heat of his body warming her cold shaking body.

Feeling Toby's cold wet nose pressing against her calf, she glanced down. "I'm okay, boy", she sniffed, reaching down to ruffle his head.

"I'll run you a bath, a long soak will warm you up, and then we'll talk". Alex spoke quietly, releasing her from his arms and heading to the stairs. "Finish that", he indicated towards the brandy. "It will help", his lopsided grin warmed Melody's heart.

Pulling the towelling robe snugly around her body, Melody headed to her bedroom. The bath, with its generous amount of lavender bubble bath Alex had run for her, had helped warm and relax her. After slipping into her silk pyjamas, she unpinned her hair, letting it cascade down her back. Alex had said they would talk after and as she worried her bottom lip, she caught sight of herself in the mirror. Her face flushed from the heat of the bath, a few tendrils of damp hair curling at her temples, wide eyes staring back at her with fear etched in them. Slipping her feet into her fluffy penguin slippers, she headed out of her room and down the stairs.

Alex looked up as Melody padded into the front room, his smile lighting his eyes. "Feeling better", he asked looking at her silk clad body, her face makeup free and flushed from the bath making her look younger and fragile, her hair falling around her shoulders in sweet curls. He resisted the urge to pull her into his arms.

Nodding, she sank into the arm chair opposite him. "I met with the local newspaper reporter Joe today, to discuss running a story on the charity gala. Remember I mentioned it to you the other day"? He paused leaning forward. "Joel and I have a plan, to flush out the thief, but it would mean involving you, would you be okay with that"?

"Yes, w-what would I have to do"? Melody stuttered, shifting uneasily in her seat.

"Well for a start, I was already intending to ask you to be my plus-one at the charity gala, and we thought you could wear the emerald necklace. Joe was going to run the story next week, but I just got off the phone with him and we've decided to run the story in a couple of days; should buy us some time. The article will describe its mysterious re-surfacing and that it is secured until then, and will be worn for all to see by you at the gala".

Melody sat motionless. "Buy us some time"? She queried looking up at Alex.

"Well, if that was the thief following you tonight, he might back off knowing what he is after is locked up elsewhere until the gala".

"And I'll be wearing it", Melody gasped, her eyes widening in fright.

"And I'll be right by your side, with all the security men keeping watch", he reassured her. Walking over to her, he squatted down in front of her. "If you don't want to do this, we will think of something else", his voice reassuring, as he reached out to hold her hands.

"No, I think we should do this", Melody stated, raising her chin in defiance. "I won't let him make me live in fear. It's a great plan, although I think we should try and meet Christina as soon as possible, let her know about it all, if she is still alive".

Alex pulled her into his arms. "I have someone working on that", he muttered.

"Me too", she smiled, as Alex raised his eyebrow in question. "I can't say how, but if I get the address tomorrow, maybe we could visit her together".

"Okay, but from now on, we don't take any chances. I'm assigning you a bodyguard from tomorrow, just till the paper runs the story".

Looking into Alex's worried eyes, Melody's refusal died on her lips; a muttered, "okay" was all she could manage. She could not fault Alex's reaction; wasn't she just as worried and knowing someone was out there, willing to break-in and now possibly follow her and maybe worse, she shuddered, a bodyguard was the lesser of two evils.

Chapter 6

Melody sat at her shop counter, absentmindedly chewing the end of her pen, watching her newly appointed bodyguard Rick, as he prowled around the shop. He had appeared that morning at the cottage to accompany her to work; her half-hearted attempt to refuse had met with Alex's firm but insistent confirmation that it was necessary for now. The moment Susie had seen him, she was all but fussing and clucking around Melody like a mother hen. The morning had flown by with Melody barely getting any work done, every time the bell above the door tinkled, she jumped like a nervous cat. Even Toby seemed to be keeping an eye on her, jumping up to follow her if she moved too far from the counter.

"It's great to have a bit of muscle around", Susie's cheerful voice pulled Melody from her thoughts. "We got those boxes up on the high shelves down", she grinned waving at Rick, as he placed one beside the counter. Opening it up, she pulled out the decorative hole punches and blank cards. "These seem to be selling well, I've had a rush on the butterfly hole punches lately", she confirmed, gesturing to the quickly forming pile, as she added another.

Picking up the pricing gun, Melody started attacking the growing pile. "I guess it's a growing trend, Suze.

Everyone wants to make their own cards". The bell above the door tinkled again and Melody almost dropped the gun.

"Oh hun, you're so jumpy", Susie tutted, reaching out her hand for the pricing gun. "I'll take that. Why don't you get some fresh air"? Glancing up from the hole punches, Melody started to refuse.

"Hi Mel", Lindsey greeted from the doorway as she headed in. "Fancy a coffee"?

"She does", Susie confirmed, nodding enthusiastically at her, "she needs to get out of here for a while. Go on Mel, I'll take care of the shop".

Walking across the road to the coffee house, she caught Lindsey's questioning arched eyebrow at Rick as he followed. "Later", she groaned, trying to impart some sense of normality into the situation. Settling down at a far booth, they ordered their coffee.

"So what gives", Lindsey whispered, flicking a glance at Rick, who had positioned himself at a table in the front of the shop.

"It's okay, Lind's, just a precaution. Alex's appointed me a bodyguard. He thinks I need to be extra careful since the break-in, and I think I was followed home last night".

"No way, did you see who"? Lindsey murmured shaking her head.

"No, just a white van; he followed me from the restaurant. When I turned into my cul-de-sac, he parked outside the turning and doused his lights. I'm probably just over-reacting", shrugging, Melody took a sip of her coffee.

"There was a white van parked next to me at the restaurant last night, Mel. The guy in it gave me the creeps; I felt like he was watching me. I thought I was being paranoid but what if..".

Melody leaned forward urgently. "Could you describe him, Lind's? Age, hair-colour, anything"? Her eyes pleading, sitting back.

Lindsey closed her eyes frowning, "Well, he looked to be in his late forties, early fifties. He had lank brown, jaw length hair, sallow skin, oh and his eyes", she shivered, "they were deep green, mean looking eyes. I couldn't tell his height as he was sitting in the van but he seemed slim built". Sighing and opening her eyes, Lindsey took Melody's hand. "That's all I can remember, sorry. I'm glad you have Rick", she glanced nervously at the bodyguard.

"Oh, that's great, Lind's. It will give us something to go on", Melody smiled encouragingly, biting down her nerves as her mind worked overtime on this new piece of information. "So how did it go at work", she whispered, watching as Lindsey drank her coffee.

Leaning in closer, Lindsey lowered her voice. "I got Christina Trafford's address that you wanted". Reaching into her bag, she retrieved a piece of paper and slipped it across the table to Melody. "But remember, you never got it from me". Glancing at her watch, Lindsey started to rise. "I have to get back to work, they'll be wondering where I've got to. Be safe, Mel". Leaning in, she kissed her cheek. "Oh and don't tell Charlotte about your new bodyguard", she laughed, winking in conspiracy.

Melody sat in a daze; unfolding the piece of paper that Lindsey had given her, she looked at the address. So Christina is alive and she wasn't too far away, maybe a ten-minute drive. With excitement bubbling inside, she pulled her bag towards herself. Grabbing her phone out, she scrolled through her contacts. "Alex", she sighed, as she found his number. Sliding further into the corner of the booth, she hit the call button.

Ordering another coffee, Melody pulled out the journal from her bag. Removing the letters from the cover, she opened the envelope. Spreading the letter, she looked at the writing penned across the page, its small cursive style handwriting in short sentences, so different from the swirling script of the journal's entries and the other letter.

June 7th 1953

Dear Christina,

Happy birthday, my sweetheart. I have missed you so much. I am finally able to write to let you know my circumstances have changed. For the past few months, I have gained employment at my uncle's business at the docks. He is pleased with my work saying often I have a flair for business and now is talking of making me his business partner. It is a modest business, and I can offer you a good life now. I await your response, my love.

Jack

Melody replaced the letter into the envelope. Turning the pages of the journal, she skimmed her eyes over the entries, not sure what she was looking for, a tear-stained page catching her eye, she stopped. Running her finger over the ink smudges, the words still legible, she began to read.

August 12th 1952

"My heart is broken, for today I discovered Jack's true reason for disappearing. I shall try to write what happened today, although difficult, with my tears blurring my vision. I had been out in the garden enjoying a walk in the sunshine when I heard raised voices from within the library. I crept closer to the open French doors where I heard Uncle James and father arguing over some heirloom that has gone missing. Uncle James was insisting father involve the police, saying it was his birth right too and as such, he should have some say in the matter, that the stable boy should be hunted down and brought to justice for the theft!

Turning, I made to run to the gardens to escape the words still ringing in my ears, and bumped straight into Philip. He looked straight at me and then the French doors knowing instantly I had overheard. His pompous, overbearing look of glee made my skin crawl. He pointed his cane at me. "Well, well, my dear cousin finally realised what a thieving scoundrel your stable boy is", he crowed at me, repetitiously rubbing his cane's silver lion head handle. "He only ever wanted you to line his own pockets. I guess the emerald heirloom was too much for him to resist, stealing it from around your neck and then leaving you for dead, and on your birthday", his scornful voice still rings in my ears.

I insisted that Jack wouldn't do that, he just couldn't, I pleaded but this just seemed to make him more insistent.

"Oh but he did, dear cousin and your father cannot pursue him for fear of humiliation and ruining your reputation. After all, it was your involvement in a secret rendezvous with this scoundrel that gave him the opportunity; he didn't stick around, did he? If innocent, he would have, you silly little girl. If he cared one little bit for you, he would have been at your side".

He raised his cane, his face contorted in rage and for one awful moment, I thought he would strike me, but just as quickly his face changed to concern, a smile on his lips, his eyes darting past me. I turned to see father approaching. "Do not speak of this to your father, he has been hurt by your silly antics enough", he growled at me, and on seeing father's white drawn face as he approached, I had no choice but to concede. How I made it to my room without letting my tears fall, I still do not know but knowing Jack has left me and stolen the necklace seems too much to bear. Maybe that's why I still can't remember; my doctor says some memories are too painful for the mind to tolerate and so we simply block them out. I re-read the note arranging for Jack and I to meet that evening and I cannot deny what Philip has said. My heart is broken, but Philip is right on one thing. I cannot cause father and mother any more pain, so will try my best to compose myself for them. I will not speak of Jack again. I will be the perfect daughter and hopefully one day my heart will heal".

Christina

Melody closed the journal, tears in her eyes for Christina's plight. If Jack had stolen the necklace, how had it ended up inside a secret pocket of the gown? Frowning at unanswered questions swirling around in her head, Melody placed the journal back into her bag and headed out of the coffee house.

The afternoon in the shop dragged on and by closing time, Melody felt relief to be heading home. As she locked up, Rick chatted to her about the day, his quick check of her car and the familiar surrounding area feeling strange to her over wrought mind.

"So once I've seen you safely inside the cottage, I'll be stationed outside in the car till Alex returns", he informed her as he opened the door to her car.

"Sure thing and Rick", she hesitated as he leaned in, "thank you". He nodded and gently closed her car door.

Standing under the powerful shower, Melody felt the day's tensions easing, as the water sluiced over her tired body. The call to Alex from the coffee house re-played over in her mind, his concerned voice reassuring her that he would investigate this new lead and reminding her to be safe and to keep Rick close. Smiling, as memories of his concern washed over her, he really did seem to care. It was a lovely feeling to be cared for, she mused. Cutting the water off and wrapping her towel securely around herself, she grabbed her pile of clothes and headed to her room.

They would be driving to Christina's home later and she felt excitement build as she opened her wardrobe to select something to wear. Pulling a dove grey jersey dress out, she had bought this dress on a whim, it was so unlike her usual attire. She ran her hand over the ever so soft material, holding it up to herself, she smiled. Yes, this would be perfect, for meeting Christina. Once dressed she pulled her curls into a high ponytail and applied a touch of makeup. Adding a pale pink belt and matching ballet pumps to finish the look. A simple gold necklace with a star pendant the only jewellery she wore nestling at the hollow in her neck. Melody gazed at herself, the knee length dress clung to her curves, revealing her slim legs. Doubt crept over her; maybe she should wear something else. She glanced back at her wardrobe biting her lip, the doorbell ringing pulled Melody from her thoughts. Grabbing a pair of delicate gold star earrings, she started to put them in as she hurried down the stairs.

Flinging the front door open, Alex's frame filled the space. "No safety chain on, Mel", he admonished, his lop-sided grin softening his words as he squinted, the sunlight temporarily blinding him.

"Oh, I forgot", she grimaced, standing back to allow him in. Closing the door, she turned to him. His eyes now focused on her jersey clad body, she felt herself blushing.

"You look beautiful", his low growl of approval making her glad she hadn't changed her dress. Taking a step closer, he reached out and pulled her into his arms, the smell of his aftershave and soap intoxicating her senses, his charcoal trousers and suit jacket bringing out the blue in his eyes. Resting a hand on his chest, Melody felt his strong heartbeat beneath the crisp white shirt. The first three buttons open, revealing a sprinkling of dark hair.

"You look good too", she muttered, reaching up to trace his strong jaw. Bending his head down, he captured her lips hungrily, parting them to explore inside, a low moan escaping her lips as he stepped back.

"I've booked us a table at Bella Aroma", he smiled down at her, tucking an escaped curl behind her ear. Glancing at his watch, he added. "After that, I thought we'd drive to Christina's to introduce ourselves. I phoned her this afternoon and she was quite intrigued to meet us". Smoothing her hands over her hips, she stepped back. "Let me just check on Toby and grab my bag". Reluctantly, he stepped aside as she made her way past him and towards the kitchen.

Alex parked his ford SUV close to the restaurant's exit. She smiled at his choice. "Quick getaway", she laughed as they walked into the restaurant. He quirked his eyebrow at her teasing and playfully smacked her bottom. "You never know, little minx", he donned a look of conspiracy, which sent her into a fit of giggles.

Seated in a secluded booth at the back of the restaurant, Melody looked over the menu as Alex ordered her a white wine and a sparkling water for himself, his deep voice settling her overly anxious nerves.

"What do you fancy", he asked as his hooded eyes roved over her face. You, she thought, biting her lip as she tried to concentrate on the menu.

"I'll have the creamy Tagliatelle and meatballs, it sounds nice", she smiled up at the waiter and closed her menu.

"Make that two", Alex announced to the waiter. As he headed away with their order, Alex leaned in taking a sip of his water. "So Mel, did you bring the journal to show Christina"?

"I did", she nodded, tapping her bag beside her.

"Good, she will probably want to see it. Her name's Christina Alexander Trafford now; she has three children, two boys, Luke and Peter, and a girl, Elizabeth. Her husband died last year from a stroke. Her eldest son Luke, has recently had Trafford manor refurbished and modernised, hence the estate sale, but that's as much as I know". He sat back, watching Melody's face as emotions played across it.

"I wonder if they knew the trunk they sold included Christina's journals. I was thinking of giving it back to her, after all, it is rightfully hers", she spoke so quietly, he had to lean in closer to hear.

"If that's what you want, although I will confirm with her that the necklace will be returned to her after the gala. After all, we need it to flush out the thief for her sake as much as ours".

Melody nodded. "When will the paper run the story"?

Alex lowered his voice. "The story runs in tomorrow's edition. We will, of course let Christina know that as well".

"And at least then, I won't need my bodyguard".

"We'll see", Alex sighed.

The waiter appeared at that moment, stopping any further discussion, placing their plates in front of them. Melody eyed her meal, her appetite suddenly deserting her.

"Mm, it's good", Alex murmured appreciatively, scooping up another meatball. Swirling some pasta around her fork, Melody glanced across at Alex, his twinkling grey-blue eyes holding hers. He looked so carefree and happy, she could not help but smile; his mood was infectious.

They were both silent on the drive to Christina's. Leaving the busy town, they were soon driving down country lanes with fields of green, some with cattle grazing as far as the eye could see. As they approached a small lane, Alex slowed the SUV and turned in. The winding lane seemed to envelop them, its towering trees on either side, making it feel more like a tunnel. After what seemed like forever, they came to a stop at the end of the lane. A pair of black wrought iron gates stood shut, barring the way. Alex hopped out and walked over to the intercom. A moment later, the big gates whirred to life, slowly opening to permit them entrance.

Shifting in his seat, he reached out his hand to caress Melody's cheek. "Here we go Mel, ready"?

"Ready as I'll ever be", she gulped. "Let's do this", she spoke, trying to sound confident.

"That's my girl, just remember, I'll be right by your side". Slipping the SUV in gear, they headed up the winding driveway. The palatial home loomed ahead of them, its white walls and columns glinting orange hues as the sunset washed over it.

Stepping out onto the cobbled stone circular driveway, Melody made her way towards the fountain. She had seen it as they had driven up the drive. Taking a closer look, the two stone dolphins entwined as if in mid jump, water spouting from their mouths. She glanced up at Alex as he reached her side. "Beautiful, isn't it", she sighed, trailing her fingers in the clear water.

"Mm, beautiful", Alex said, looking into her eyes. She smiled shyly at him; he always did this to her, made her feel she was the only thing he could see. "Let's go say hello", he murmured, wrapping his arm around her shoulders and leading her around the fountain to the steps of the entrance and the large glass filled front door. As Alex pressed the brass bell, the high pitched ring seemed to echo through Melody. She leaned in a little closer to Alex; his response a gentle squeeze was all she needed. Movement inside the door caught her attention; just then as the door opened, a plump lady with rosy cheeks stood looking out at them.

"Christina um Lady Alexander 'Trafford", Alex asked.

She shook her head. "No, I'm Anne, is she expecting you"?

"I spoke to her on the phone earlier today. I'm Alex Knight and this is Melody Croft", he motioned towards Melody. Melody watched as the lady's face softened and smiled at them, rubbing her hands on her apron.

"Oh yes, come on in, she's been expecting you", she muttered, standing back to let them pass. Leading them through a grand hallway, her black court shoes silent on the high shine marble floor, walking around a stunning curved duel staircases, a large chandelier hanging directly above it picking out the gold fleur-de-lis pattern in the royal blue carpet lining the stairs, its magnificence not lost on Melody as she romanticised walking down one side of it, dressed in a gown running her fingers over the highly polished mahogany handrail with Alex waiting for her at the bottom dressed in a tux. "Here we are", Anne's voice jerked Melody back from her daydream as she briskly ushered them into a spacious room.

"Lady Alexander 'Trafford, your guests, Mr Knight and Ms Croft", she announced, sweeping her arm towards them.

"Thank you Anne". Turning to her guests, she beckoned them in. "Please take a seat", she motioned for them to sit. Taking a seat on a large ivory coloured baroque sofa that Lady Alexander 'Trafford had indicated to them, Melody felt the cool silk against the backs of her legs making her unconsciously pull at the hem of her dress.

"Would you care for some tea", she asked looking from Melody to Alex.

"That would be lovely, Lady Alexander 'Trafford", Alex accepted, as he rested back on the sofa.

"Oh, please call me Christina", she smiled at him.

"Well, it's nice to meet you Christina, I'm Alex", pausing, he flicked a glance at Melody, "and this is Melody. She's the one who purchased your old trunk and found the journals".

Christina's eyes flicked to where Anne still stood hovering. "We'll have that tea now, please Anne".

As Melody looked around the room, the glass windows reflected the glow of several lamps scattered around, mingling with the orangey hues of the sunset bathing the room in a warm glow. Huge pot plants strategically placed on each side of the doors, the same baroque style coffee table in the centre perched on a gold and cream silk Indian rug, enhancing the gold of the woodwork on the sofas and table, its opulence radiating over Melody. Turning her attention to Christina who was sitting regally on a smaller baroque sofa, her small frame encased in a soft oatmeal coloured cashmere sweater and skirt, her silver grey hair pinned up in a chignon, a simple pearl necklace and matching earrings her only accessories.

"Ah, there you are, Anne", Christina's greeting pulled Melody back from her musings, "there will be fine, thank you", she pointed towards the coffee table as Anne placed the tea tray down, the fine bone china tea set clinking gently. When Anne left, she turned to her guests. "Well, I must say I was surprised when I got your call. Of course I knew my son organised the estate sale, but I never once thought about my old gowns or journals turning up". Pausing, she poured the tea. "Help yourselves to milk and sugar", she smiled, waving her hand at the tray.

Melody reached into her bag and pulled out the journal. "Here's the journal we mentioned, there were three of them", she said handing over the journal to Christina. "I was burgled and the thief took the other two, but luckily I had that one with me".

Turning the pages of the journal, Christina's eyes misted, a gentle sigh escaping. "It's been so long since I've seen this". Taking the letters out, she lovingly opened them. "So long", she sighed again.

"Did you ever see Jack again"? Melody asked, leaning forward, gazing at the far off look in Christina's eyes.

"No, he never did come back", waving at the letters, she added, "after my party it came to light that he had stolen something valuable from me, an heirloom. My father and mother would never speak of it, and when he sent this other letter, they hid it from me for years. When I discovered the letter, it was too late; my father was ill and I was newly married. I couldn't bring myself to re-open those old wounds; I never will understand why he sent it".

"Did you ever regain your memories"? Alex asked, his voice soft.

"Some but nothing of consequence", she sighed, as her shoulders slumped slightly.

"When I was unpicking your gown, I found a hidden pocket". Melody paused, looking into Christina's watery eyes. "I found an emerald and diamond necklace, was that what you thought Jack had stolen"?

"Was it a g-gold gown"? Christina stammered, her eyes wide with shock.

"Yes it was", Melody nodded.

Collapsing back onto the sofa, Christina raised her hand to her head, fingering a faint white scar on her forehead. "I have visions of that gown. I could never quite capture the memory, but I must have put it there. Oh god, Jack was innocent", she gasped, the letters falling to the floor.

Melody quickly went to her, kneeling down, retrieving the letters and placing them on the coffee table. Taking Christina's frail hands in her own, "I'm so sorry", she breathlessly stated, squeezing Christina's hands.

"It's okay dear, just...", she stopped mid-sentence, frowning at Alex as he picked up the letters and studied them, his frown deepening. "W-what's wrong", she stuttered, her green eyes sharply focused on his face.

"These letters, you say Jack penned them both"?

"Yes, what of it"?

Waving the letters, he looked at Melody. "It's just they are both so different. I never noticed this before, the note requesting you meet on the eve of your party is in bold swirling script, while the other letter is in small cursive handwriting, so different", he paused handing them the letters to inspect, "something seems off to me", he stated rubbing his jaw.

"I never compared them before, but if he didn't write one or both, who did"? Christina asked, looking uncertainly at them.

"I think whoever wants this necklace is playing a very devious game, the later letter with Jack's full name and address in the corner", he pointed at it, "I believe to be real that there was indeed a Jack Turner living at that address at the time it was written. The note on the eve of your party, however, I believe was not written by him". Pausing, he looked between the two of them. "I think it was written by somebody you know, and was deliberately used to lure you away from the party to steal the necklace and set Jack up".

"But they never got the necklace, did they"? Melody mused aloud.

"No, but they let Jack take the fall to cover themselves, and I'm sure whoever is after it now knows all about it, and thinks the journals hold the key to finding it".

"W-what will we do", Christina croaked, her hands shaking.

Melody gently rubbed her hand on Christina's hands. "It's okay, please don't fret. We have a plan", she soothed, looking to Alex for help.

For the next half hour, Alex filled Christina in on the plans, explaining about the newspaper article being published the following day and the gala they would attend, with Melody wearing the necklace to flush out the thief with Christina's permission. With her heartfelt plea to be safe and not take unnecessary risks, she agreed to the plan. After assuring her of the safety precautions and promising to keep her informed, Alex assured her that they would do all they could to exonerate Jack.

As they made to leave, Alex stopped in the entranceway. Grabbing a notebook and pen from his jacket pocket and writing his number down, he smiled reassuringly at Christina. "If you think of anything or need help in anyway, don't hesitate to call me anytime". Placing the number in her hands, he reiterated, "Anytime".

"Wait, you forgot something", Christina sighed placing her hand on Melody's arm. "The journal, you left it in the conservatory".

Turning to go and retrieve it, Melody reached out to stop her. "It's okay, Christina. I meant to say earlier, I'm leaving it with you, it is after all rightfully yours".

Turning back with tears in her eyes, she took hold of Melody's hands. "Bless you dear, that really is kind".

Watching them drive away, her mind wandering over all that had happened, she felt a glimmer of hope. Could they really solve this mystery of who set Jack up, and if they did, would she finally be able to meet again with her beloved Jack?

Chapter 7

Melody sat at her shop counter, the morning's paper spread before her, the picture of the Emerald necklace staring back at her. The headline, *'MISSING HEIRLOOM MYSTERIOUSLY RETURNS',* catching her eye, sipping her coffee, she read on.

'The Trafford Emerald necklace has mysteriously returned! After many years of speculation of its unconfirmed disappearance, we have now been informed of its reappearance. Having been in the Trafford's possession since 1853 and passed down for generations, this heirloom is purported to hold mystical properties bestowing on the owner power and wealth. Sources say it is being held under tight security at an undisclosed location. It has been confirmed that permission has been granted for it to be worn by Melody Croft, the lady responsible for finding it, for all to see for the first time in years at the Crafton hotel on the evening of the Hopes & Dreams charity gala, these highly sort after tickets are selling fast so...'

Melody stopped reading, her heart pounding fast. So it was done, she would wear the necklace for all to see. The plan was in motion, now what to wear, she mused, worrying her bottom lip, her mind turning to the rose-pink gown at home as a plan started to take root.

"Susie, I'm just stepping out for a few minutes", she called out, grabbing her bag and heading to the door. "No, you stay, boy", she commanded Toby, rubbing his head and pointing him back to his bed, as Rick sidled up to her.

"Where to, Mel", he inquired, opening the door for her.

"Just popping to the material shop, you don't have to come, I'm sure I'll be fine".

Shaking his head, he stepped outside the shop with her. "Best if I come. Alex would skin me alive if anything happened to you". Smiling, he fell into step beside her.

The day had been a busy one between customers coming in and asking all about the newspaper article, and Melody's phone ringing all day with inquisitive friends not to mention several calls from Sarah checking up on her. It's a wonder she'd managed to get any work done.

The relief of stepping into her quiet cottage felt like a balm to her frayed nerves. Pouring some kibble into Toby's bowl and then flicking on the coffee machine, Melody sat at the kitchen table, the paper bag from the material shop propped up on the chair beside her. Reaching over to it, she pulled the material out, lovingly fingering the yards of black Venetian lace, a quiet evening designing and sewing was just what she needed. Scooping up the lace, she headed across the kitchen to her craft room, placing the material on her cutting table. She spun round to look at the rose-pink gown, the sleeveless fitted satin bodice and drop waist flaring to a full tulle skirt would be perfect, she mused. Detaching the old fashioned rosebuds from around the neckline and the few scattered at the front hem shouldn't be too problematic. Tilting her head, she envisioned the black Venetian lace fitted over the bodice and dropped waist, the pink peeking through the swirls in the lace would look stunning.

Placing the dress on the mannequin, she started the laborious task of unpicking the rosebuds. Much later, as she kneeled in front of the dress, Melody unpicked the last rosebud. Sitting back on her heels, she stretched her aching back, dropping the last one onto the small pile of rosebuds beside her on the floor. She looked at the dress, pleased with its progress. Toby prowling in caught her eye; he sniffed at the pile inquisitively then half climbed on her knees, pushing his nose into her hands. "Have I been neglecting you, boy", she soothed, obediently rubbing his head, as his soulful eyes looked reproachfully at her, his tail thumping happily, sending the rosebuds scattering across the floor. "Okay, I get it, boy, time for your walk, huh". Shifting him off her lap, she stood, bending down to scoop up the rosebuds. "How about we see if Alex's home and fancies a walk with us", she crooned as Toby skipped and circled excitedly around her.

As soon as they stepped out of the SUV and into the park, Toby was off running ahead of them, looking excitedly back at Alex, readying himself for his ball to be thrown. She loved coming here to walk Toby, the winding pathway secluded away from the road by large trees to one side with bluebells clustered beneath them, open fields sprawled on the other side, the long grass no obstacle for Toby as he hunted for his ball.

Melody glanced at Alex, the evening sun picking out the planes and grooves of his face, the breeze catching at his dark brown hair styled in a slick back undercut, ruffling it against his forehead as he absentmindedly raked his fingers through it pushing it back off his face, his strong jaw shadowed with stubble, the cleft in his chin barely visible, long legs encased in black denim, a black t-shirt tucked into his jeans. Watching as he bent to retrieve Toby's ball and throw it again for him, she admired his taut muscles flexing in his arms, a contented sigh escaping her.

"Penny for them", Alex laughed, reaching for her hand. He always loved the way she blushed whenever he caught her staring.

"I um, was just wondering what Christina will do with the necklace when she finally gets it back", she answered linking her fingers into Alex's.

"I guess she will pass it onto one of her children, eventually", he mused stopping to throw the ball again.

"I wouldn't want it if I was her with all that has happened to her because of it", she sighed, a look of worry in her eyes.

"It will be fine, Mel". Looking at her puzzled frown, he continued. "The gala, you will be safe. You know, we'll have our best men working security, and I'll be right by your side".

"Have you had any luck tracing Jack yet"?

"We have a couple of promising leads, hopefully we'll have something concrete soon". Cupping her face in his hands, he looked into her eyes. The sun catching at the flecks of gold turning them to pools of amber, a scattering of freckles across her nose making her look younger, vulnerable almost. "What'd you say to picking up a takeaway on the way home", his voice sounding gruff to his own ears as he tucked a wayward curl behind her ear.

"Sounds great, and I have some ice-cream left over in the freezer from last time, which I know you're rather partial to", she teased.

"Okay minx, let's head back to the SUV. I'm starving", he grinned.

Timothy slammed the newspaper down on the small table, glaring at the article on the emerald necklace. It was so close, he could almost taste his victory. So the third journal must have held the key to the missing heirloom and now for the time being, it was out of his reach, and some common girl would be wearing it at the gala, his mouth sneering at the distasteful thought. Now all he needed was a ticket to the event, scanning the article for the date and location. His eyes narrowed in displeasure as he saw the price of a ticket. There was no way his meagre budget would stretch to this, let alone the tux he would have to hire.

Leaning back in his chair, he looked around his bedsit; the peeling wallpaper and shabby carpet seemed to mock him, the single bed and wardrobe the only other furniture in the small room, a far cry from Trafford Manor. It should have been his father's and then his, he fumed slamming his fist against the table. Memories of his father's tales flooded him, tales of how his great grandmother having always favourited her younger son, Edward, had cut her firstborn son James, from his inheritance of Trafford Manor, placing the title and all its spoils to Edward. "Just because of a few gambling debts", his father would bellow. Never letting him forget that even as far as favouring Edwards's wife over his own grandmother and giving her the heirloom, when that too should have gone to his grandmother, his grandfather demoted to working for one of his father's smaller holdings, a position just above a servant, he sneered at the thought.

Picking up his mobile phone, he checked the remaining credit on it. Just enough, he thought, selecting a contact and hitting dial. "It's me", he barked into the phone.

"Timothy, what do you want? I said not to call me unless it was urgent".

"It is. I need access to the charity gala to continue our mission, can you help"? Explaining the newspaper article and price of the ticket, he waited for what seemed like forever.

"Well, well, looks like you'll have to attend in some other capacity", the harsh voice informed him.

"What other capacity"? He snarled impatiently.

"Temper, temper", the voice mocked him continuing, "I think, even you should be able to secure a position as a waiter at the event". A shocked hiss escaping his lips, his next cutting retort dying on his lips as the mocking voice continued. "So how's your dear father doing, I must call in to see him sometime"?

Cutting the call abruptly, he grabbed the paper screwing it up in his fist. Damn, he swore, throwing the crumpled newspaper at the wastepaper basket. So that's how you want to play it, he grimaced. Walking over to the wardrobe, he pulled out his one pair of smart black trousers and selected a white shirt, laying them over the chair in readiness for Monday. "Time to get an interview at the agency, one waiter coming up", he muttered, a strange smile on his face.

Charlotte sat in her car, looking out at Melody's cottage, the lights blazing, giving it a warm cosy postcard look. The black satin high heeled Jimmy Choo's she had promised to lend to Melody, sitting in a bag on the passenger seat. Grabbing them and her handbag, she headed down the path to the cottage. As she raised her hand to knock, the door flew open. Towering before her stood the most handsome man she had ever laid eyes on, his army style short jet black hair softly gelled back and startling blue eyes with long black lashes that any woman would kill for, and what a body she mused, flicking a look down his lean well-muscled frame. A sand-coloured t-shirt moulded to the contours of his broad chest, a tattoo of wings and a laurel wreath in between them on his well-defined bicep peeking out from his sleeve, tight faded blue denim jeans hugged his hips and thighs.

"Can I help you"? His deep gravelly voice snapped her attention back to his face.

"Umm, who are you? I'm here to see Melody, I've got the shoes she wanted", she gushed, waving the bag and trying to peer around his large frame.

"I'm Joel, a friend of Alex and Melody's and who may I ask are you"? He spoke, raising an inquisitive eyebrow at her. Standing, looking at her, he felt her bristle as she lifted her chin in defiance. Smoky grey almond shaped eyes stared back at him from a small oval face.

His eyes were drawn to her kissable cupid's bow lips, painted a rich pink as her tongue darted out to wet them, her small five-foot three petite frame and pink tipped spiky blonde hair making him think of an angry pixie. "My name's Charlotte. I'm Melody's best friend", she announced tightly. He almost imagined that she wanted to stamp her foot.

"Welcome, Charlotte", he gave a mock bow. "You'll find her in the kitchen", he answered, stifling a grin and waving her into the house as he stepped outside. Shaking his head as wayward thoughts of kissing that angry pixie, turning her fiery temper into passion running rampant in his head, he made his way to his van.

"Hi Mel, it's just me", she called out as she made her way down the hallway. "I just met your overbearing guard dog", she pouted, entering the kitchen, stopping mid-rant as Alex and Melody turned to look at her from their seats at the kitchen table.

"Oh no! What's Joel done now", Alex groaned, shooting Melody a quizzical look.

"Well, apart from seeming like he wanted to frisk me and take fingerprints, he's just a darling", Charlotte replied sarcastically, a smile tugging at her mouth.

"Oh Lottie, you're too much", Melody laughed as she walked over to her friend.

"He's just being overly cautious, you know, with this break-in and everything that's going on". Flinging her arms around Charlotte, she hugged her friend.

"Well I guess, but seriously, what danger would I be", she laughed, hugging Melody back and trying to make light of the situation.

"I brought you the shoes", she stepped back motioning to the bag.

"Fancy a coffee", Melody asked, taking the bag from Lottie.

"Geez, no way, I'll be up all night", she laughed, taking a seat next to Alex. "So how's the spy business going", she teased.

"The security business", he cheerfully corrected her, winking at Melody, who was well used to this game. "It's going well, why, you want a job"? He laughed.

"Uh, no thanks! So, is this Joel guy one of your security men"? Charlotte asked, her eyes darting to the hallway.

"No, he's my business partner, and don't worry, he's not coming back tonight".

Blushing at being caught out looking for him, Charlotte turned to Melody. "So what do you think of the shoes, will they go with your gown"?

Placing a mug of hot chocolate down in front of Charlotte, Melody lifted a shoe out of the bag, looking at the black satin four-inch heeled shoe, the diamantes on the heel and mini platform sparkling in the kitchen light. "Oh, they're perfect, Lottie", Melody sighed, holding it up to the light. "Come and see the gown", she gestured towards her craft room.

"Ah, so Cinderella will go to the ball", Charlotte teased, as they headed back to into the kitchen. Grabbing her hot chocolate, she looked at Alex. "So, have you seen it"?

"No, Melody wants to surprise me", he pulled a hard done by face.

"Well, she'll be the most beautiful girl at the gala", she enthused, smiling at Melody over her mug. "Will you wear a wrap with it, Mel"?

"I'm thinking of making a matching lace one, what do you think"?

"Ladies", Alex interrupted them, "I'll leave you to your girly chat, I need to pop home and make a few calls. Nice to see you again Charlotte, I'll tell Joel, you said hello", he teased, giving her his most dazzling smile as she blushed. Turning back again to Melody, he brushed a kiss on her lips. "See you in a little while", his gruff whisper giving her goosebumps, as the heat of his mouth warmed her neck.

"Well, he's a keeper", Charlotte exploded as soon as Alex had left.

Melody sat smiling at her friend's enthusiasm. "He sure is", she sighed, a dreamy look on her face.

"And you got it bad", Charlotte laughed reaching down to rub Toby's head.

"His business partner isn't bad either", Melody grinned at her friend's shocked face. "I know you too well Lottie, until Alex told you he wasn't coming back, I'm sure I caught you looking longingly at the hallway".

"Melody Croft, don't you dare start match-making", she feigned disapproval, throwing her hands in the air in surrender.

Melody laughed. "Okay Lottie, you got me, so how about I pour you a glass of wine and show you my designs for a Venetian lace wrap"?

"Wine, now you're talking Mel".

Later, after waving goodbye to Lottie and rinsing the mugs and wine glasses, Melody sat on her sofa, her feet curled under her, Toby laying tight against her silk pyjamaed legs. Every now and again, his legs twitching as if he was running after bunnies in his dreams, she smiled rubbing his head to soothe him. Glancing around the room, Melody felt content. The time spent catching up with Lottie, always left her feeling happy. The glow from the lamps casting shadows all around, the familiar figurines on the mantel piece, the old walnut clock, its scrolled feet and patina displaying the clock face perfectly, its gentle tick reminding her of evenings spent here with her grandmother.

Uncurling her legs, Melody carefully eased Toby over and stretched her legs. Looking at the bookcase, standing slightly behind the overstuffed chair, she quickly decided that a little light reading while she awaited Alex's return was just what she needed. Making her way over, she lovingly ran her fingers over the old spines. Pushing the chair over a little to reach the lower shelf and selecting a romance novel, she turned to make her way back to the sofa. Jutting out from under the chair, she noticed a little white piece of card. Stooping down, she retrieved it. Turning it over in her hand, she noted the worn business card, the corners bent and scuffed, 'A1 Employment Agency' emblazoned across the card in block letters, a green logo of a hand holding a plate with a tool belt and tools above it in the corner, phone and fax numbers inserted beneath in italics. Strange, she thought, placing it beside the clock on the mantle, "Joel or Alex must have dropped it there", she mused aloud, inching her way back on the sofa next to Toby. "It's okay boy, go back to sleep", she hushed as she rubbed his head. Flipping her book open, she soon lost herself in the story.

As Alex let himself into Melody's cottage, silence greeted him. Entering the kitchen, he found it empty; he walked into the front room. Toby lifted his head excitedly and jumped down to greet him. "Shh boy", Alex whispered as he spotted Melody curled up, fast asleep on the sofa. Taking the book from her limp hands and placing it on the coffee table, he smiled to himself noticing the title, "The Italian Rake". Turning back, he gently brushed a kiss on her forehead. She murmured something undiscernible and snuggled her face against his. Gently lifting her, he carried her upstairs to her bed, pulling the duvet over her. He glanced at her flushed face, her sweeping lashes flickering in dreams, her full mouth slightly open. Unable to resist, he placed a kiss on them. "Sweet dreams, my pretty angel", he whispered, flicking the lamp off and stopping at the door to check she was still asleep.

Chapter 8

The sun blazing through the curtains woke Melody; the bedside clock display telling her it was already past nine. Damn, she was going to be late for work; she should not have finished that bottle of wine last night, she chastised herself struggling with the duvet to get up. And how she ended up in bed, she could not remember climbing in last night. Shaking her head to clear the fog, she opened the curtains and flung the window open; a lovely summer's day greeted her, the gentle breeze ruffling her hair. She would have to call Susie and let her know she was running late, she decided as she made her way downstairs to the kitchen. A coffee was what she needed, her mouth felt so dry as if she had been chewing her pillow.

After opening the back door to let an eager Toby out, Melody headed to the coffee machine; a full jug already sat on the hotplate, propped in front was a note addressed to her.

"Morning sleepy head, I thought it best to not wake you on your day off, and you were sparked out when I carried you to bed last night, too much vino perhaps".

She could almost imagine his lop-sided smile and his grey-blue eyes crinkling with laughter at his words. Of course, no work today! She had Karren cover for her on

Saturdays, the guilt of over-sleeping evaporating. Pouring herself a coffee and sitting down at the kitchen table, she smiled at the image of Alex's cheeky smile. She imagined he would have as he wrote the note, taking a sip of her coffee she continued reading.

"I fed the monster after taking him for a run with me this morning, so you should have some peace. Sarah called to say she will be popping in to see you about eleven. She was pleased to know you were having a rare lie-in. I'll be finished with Joel and work around one. Thought you might fancy a drive in the countryside with me then. Take care my sweet, Alex x"

So, he had put her to bed, a vague memory lingered of him kissing her lips; she had thought it had been a dream. She felt herself blush at the memory.

Grabbing Toby's chew-toy, she called him in and shut the back door. "Here you go boy, chew on that", she waved it at him, playing tug until he won and headed with his prize to his bed. "Won't be long Tob's, be good", she called over her shoulder as she headed up the stairs to her room. Grabbing her towelling robe, she headed into the bathroom for a shower. Sitting at her dressing table, she combed her freshly washed hair, deciding to let it air dry. She headed over to her wardrobe and selected baby blue shorts and a white cropped t-shirt. Having finished dressing she looked at herself in the full length mirror, pleased with her newly acquired suntan. Breakfast first, then thirty minutes sunbathing and then she would get to work on her niece's dress, she promised herself, grabbing the sun cream and heading downstairs.

She was twirling around, her rose pink gown swirling around her feet, the familiar music echoing hauntingly around her, dancers twirling by, their faces a blur, the shadowy figure looming closer and closer as each couple passed her by. The music tempo speeding up, a feeling of breathlessness gripping her, she wanted to stop dancing, fear building inside as the shadowy figure drew closer, something silver glinting menacingly in his black gloved hand. If only she could see his face but all that was there was an empty space. Suddenly the music stopped, and the figure loomed over her, his hand raised over her, about to strike the silver object poised above her head, the face of a lion bearing down, a strangled scream ripped from her throat. Melody woke with a start. Toby sat with his paw on her stomach, his soulful eyes looking anxiously at her. "It's okay boy, just a nightmare", she shakily reassured him, glancing warily around the empty garden from her sun lounger. No ghouls lurking here, she chastised herself, her mouth suddenly dry. "How about a drink, Tob's", she cajoled, walking into the kitchen, pouring fresh water into his bowl and then grabbing a can of lemonade from the fridge. Scooping out a couple of biscuits from Toby's treat jar and popping them down for him, "good boy", she praised, dropping down to hug him.

Taking a swallow of her lemonade, she made her way into the craft room, her eyes adjusting from the brightness of the garden. Now to work, she mused, picking up the gold party dress she was sewing for Lucy. The little puff sleeves and scooped neck edged with ribbon picked to match the blue-green embroidered flowers, the cut-away full skirt revealing the blue-green tulle she had pinned there. "Time to sew you in". Placing it on the sewing machine, she got to work.

Cutting the cotton, Melody pulled the dress onto a clothes hanger. Standing back to check her work, "it's missing something", she mused, tilting her head sideways and biting her lip. "A sash". Clapping her hands in delight, she picked up the reel of blue-green ribbon, pinning it around the waist, below the zipper and tying a large bow at the back. "Perfect", she muttered, taking it back to the sewing machine to fix it in place.

Re-hanging it on the clothes hanger, she stood back once again, imagining Lucy wearing it. Cutting two lengths of the blue-green ribbon for Lucy's hair to finish the look, she hung them with the dress. Toby's barking brought Melody to the kitchen. Just as she was about to tell him to be quiet, the doorbell chimed. Glancing at the clock, she groaned. "Oh, it's eleven already, that'll be Sarah". Hurrying to the door, she paused, feeling foolish. She put the safety chain on first, peering round the door as she opened it a crack. Melody saw Sarah and Lucy standing there.

"Oh, I'm so glad to see you're using it", Sarah enthused as Lucy fidgeted excitedly by her side. Opening the door wide, she let them in.

"Where's Tobee", Lucy asked dancing down the hall; hearing his name, he came rushing from the kitchen. "Aww, Tobee, I missed you". Throwing her arms around his neck as he happily greeted her, little squeals of delight escaped Lucy as he licked her.

"Show him the toy we bought him Luce", Sarah cajoled, pulling a squeaky toy from her bag and handing it to her as they headed into the kitchen.

"It's name's Dino, cos it's a dinosaur", Lucy informed Toby in a sing song voice, holding the orange toy out for him to sniff. "Can we play in the garden, mummy"?

"Sure Luce, if it's ok with aunty Mel". Turning big green pleading eyes to Melody, Lucy hopped up and down.

"Sure, munchkin, have fun", Melody smiled, watching her little niece as she headed outside chatting excitedly to Toby.

"Fancy a coffee, sis"? Melody offered, busily collecting mugs from the cupboard.

"Oh yes, please! So tell me, how's the party dress coming on"?

"Just a few embellishments left to sew on and it will be done. Oh and I bought some adorable gold sparkly ballet pumps to go with it, she'll look perfect".

"You're the best aunty". Placing the mugs down on the table, Melody sat down eyeing her sister.

"So sis, what's up, you look sad". Casting a wary eye towards the backdoor, she lowered her voice. "It's Rich, I think he's cheating on me".

Melody felt her skin crawl at the mention of Richard, her sister's husband. They had an awkward relationship since he had first married her sister; he walked around like he was god's gift, not that he was unattractive. She could see why her sister had fallen for him; slim built with short dark hair and chocolate brown eyes, charm oozing out from every pore. But the cracks had started to show almost immediately to Melody, as he started unashamedly flirting with her whenever Sarah's back was turned, his suggestive comments to her always just above reproach, her rebuffs falling on deaf ears, leaving Melody in the unenviable situation of having nothing concrete to pin on him. So keeping quiet and avoiding him as much as she could without arousing suspicion, was her only option not to hurt her sister.

"Are you sure? What makes you think that"? Melody asked, keeping her tone as neutral as possible.

"Well, it's a feeling I guess. Lots of little things really, he's been spending extra time at the gym, staying late at work, even buying younger style clothes as if he's trying to impress someone. If I try to question him about it, he starts an argument".

"Maybe it's just a mid-life crisis", Melody offered charitably.

"I hoped that too, but then I found this". Pulling a receipt from her bag, Sarah handed it to her. A receipt from Bella Aroma detailing a meal for two, very incriminating she mused to herself. "But that's not all", Sarah sighed resignedly, "there was a charge on the credit card dating back to last month from the florists, I never received any flowers".

Melody jumped up from her seat. "Oh love", she soothed, wrapping her arms around her sister. "I'm sure there's a perfectly good reason for all this". Even as the words left her mouth, Melody doubted their validity.

"Wass wrong, mummy", Lucy's cry from the door, cutting off Sarah's tears instantly.

"Mummy's fine munchkin, just needed a cuddle", Melody spoke softly, smiling reassuringly at her niece. Sarah responded by opening her arms to Lucy, who quickly ran across the kitchen and launched into her arms. "I bet all that playing in the garden has left you thirsty munchkin, want one of my special orange juice drinks"?

Wide eyes turned to Melody. "Yes please". Reaching into the fridge, she pulled out a juice box.

"Here you go, munchkin. One special juice for a special girl". Handing it to her, Melody glanced at Sarah, an unspoken thank you written over her face. Later, as Melody hugged them both goodbye with a promise to call soon, she watched them as they drove away, tears filling her eyes for her sister's plight.

Standing in the kitchen, chopping vegetables and adding them to her slow cook, she stirred the vegetables and diced lamb, sprinkling in some herbs, the casserole's aromas already filling the small kitchen. Melody contentedly hummed along to the radio, her earlier gloomy mood evaporating with the sunshine and promise of spending an afternoon with Alex. Pulling the peach cobbler from the oven and setting it on a heat mat, Melody smiled as Toby hungrily eyed the dish. "Oh no, don't you get any ideas. This is dinner for Alex and me", she laughingly fluffed his ears as he hopefully sniffed the air.

"Who's getting ideas", Alex's rumble of laughter from the doorway made her jump.

"Oh, just Tob's, trying his luck with our dessert". Recovering fast and gesturing to the cobbler.

"Can't blame him Mel, it smells so good in here". Reaching her side and pulling her into his arms, he rubbed flour off her nose with his thumb. "Flour suits you, though", his eyes hungrily devouring her as she absentmindedly brushed her fingers over her face to remove any remaining flour.

"I've put a lamb casserole on in the slow cook for later", she stated, stepping back and unfastening her apron. "So, how was work".

Pulling a piece of paper from his jacket pocket and waving it at her. "Got a promising lead on Jack, thought we could swing by this address on our drive". Clasping her hands excitedly, she nodded. "How's your day been? Apart from all the cooking", he grinned.

Filling him in on her day, she finished with Sarah's news about Richard. "I just don't know what to do for her", she confessed hopelessly.

"I could look into it for you", he suggested lifting her chin up to look into her eyes. "But you'd have to get Sarah's permission, and she might not like what I find".

"You'd really do that for us"? Winding her arms around his neck, she pulled his head lower, placing a kiss on his lips. "Thank you", her voice was husky with emotion.

"Joel knows a guy who would be perfect for the job, but like I said, Mel, you must get Sarah's permission before we do".

"I will", she promised, tilting her head and worrying her lower lip as she remembered the agency card on the mantel.

"Have you lost a business card by any chance" she asked, looking at his puzzled face she stepped away and went to retrieve it. "A1 Employment Agency", she read aloud, walking back in and handing it to him.

"No, it's not mine", he frowned studying it.

"Maybe its Joel's then, I found it under the arm chair last night, and it's not mine".

"I'll ask Joel tomorrow, it's probably his", he surmised, slipping it into his wallet.

The drive into the country was a pleasant one. Stopping at a little pub to have some lunch in the beer garden while Toby munched on their left over crusts of bread, closing her eyes and lifting her face to the sun, Melody enjoyed the warmth of the sunshine, the sound of children playing in the beer garden washing over her.

"According to the sat-nav, Jack's address is just five minutes away", Alex's voice broke the spell. Peeking between her lashes, she watched him tapping on his mobile phone.

"You think he really lives there", the hopeful lilt in her voice not lost on Alex.

"Well, there's only one way to find out", he stood, reaching for her hand. Taking his hand and rising out of her seat, she motioned for Toby to follow.

"I've got a good feeling about this", she whispered as they walked back to the SUV.

They sat parked across the road, looking at the sprawling bungalow, the winding driveway leading to a bright buttercup yellow front door surrounded by honeysuckle. The orange-red flowers blanketing the stone siding walls, the matching wooden window frames reflecting the sun, full flower boxes sat on each window ledge, a riot of colours spilling from them. The front garden was left wild and rambling, a few hens scattered around scratching at the ground. To the left of the driveway, a large oak tree sat in the middle of the lawn, an old rope swing swaying gently in the breeze.

"It looks magical", Melody breathed, turning in her seat to get a better look.

"We'd better leave Toby here, can't have him chasing the hens", Alex mused, opening the windows a crack. "Can't have you over-heating, can we boy". Leaning his hand back to ruffle Toby.

Lifting the iron knocker, Melody had a feeling of De-ja-vu. "Here we go again", Alex muttered, as if reading her mind. The knock seemed to vibrate through the bungalow. "Show time", Alex whispered, reaching for her hand as the door opened a crack. Wary old eyes peered out at them.

"Yes", a rather croaky voice inquired.

"Hello sir, are you by any chance Jack Turner".

"Who's asking".

Alex stepped forward, sweeping his arm towards Melody. "This is Melody Croft and I'm Alex Knight. We're acquaintances of Lady Christina Alexander' Trafford". Silence loomed and for a minute, Melody thought the door was going to be shut in their faces.

Suddenly the door swung wide, revealing a tall old man, a hesitant smile on his wrinkled face, twinkling soft blue eyes skimming over them, a full head of white hair and moustache belied his age. "You say you know Christina"?

"Yes sir, and she wants to rectify a terrible wrong she believes has been done to you", Alex's sincere voice seemed to stir something in Jack as he stepped back.

"Best you come in then, lad", he said, waving them in.

Walking them through the wide hallway and past a large console table groaning with photo frames standing against the wall, smiling faces of growing children and adults, spanning the years depicted a large happy family. As they stepped into the kitchen, Jack motioned for them to take a seat at the old butcher's block kitchen table. Retrieving a jug of cloudy lemonade and three glasses, he placed them on the table.

"Help yourselves", indicating the drink, he sank down onto a chair. Melody poured out the drinks, glancing around the old kitchen. The scrubbed surfaces and cupboards looked well used and worn, a shelving unit stood by the back door full of plant cuttings in yoghurt pots and small containers. Flicking a glance to the windows, she noted an assortment of teapots lining the windowsill, each with a plant spouting out from where the lid would have once been. "Me wife always said I had green fingers", Jack smiled, nodding at the teapots.

"You like them lass".

"They're lovely, Mr Turner". Turning back to him, her smile was slightly sad. "My grandmother had green fingers too, she always had cuttings growing on the windowsill".

"Had? I take it she's passed", he stated, looking at Melody. She inclined her head, biting her quivering lip. "I'm sorry lass, it gets easier you know. I lost me wife a few years ago, still expect her to walk in and tell me off about something", his eyes wistful at the memory "and call me Jack lass. Mr Turner makes me feel like me father", his voice gruff as if trying to keep his emotions in check. "So tell me about Christina, it's been so long since I've heard her name", he motioned to Alex.

Alex spoke softly, telling Jack of the night of Christina's party, the note supposedly from Jack arranging to meet, the attack and subsequent memory loss, how Melody had found the journals and the missing heirloom. Pausing briefly, he looked across at Jack, shock and sadness written all over the old man's face. Deciding he could trust Jack, he divulged a little of their plan to flush out the thief.

All the while, Jack sat motionless absorbing all the news. "I never understood why I was dismissed that day, just a curt note telling me to clear out my things and be gone", Jack spoke quietly as if lost in the past. "I wrote to Christina later, but she never replied. I just assumed what we'd had, had been one-sided". He cast a forlorn gaze at Melody.

"She never received that letter until years later", Melody sighed, the hopelessness of the past hurts they had endured, saddening her. "She did love you though, Jack", her voice was hesitant, as she reached out to rub his hand. "She went to the library to meet you that night".

"Thank you lass", Jack mumbled, patting Melody's hand. Frowning, he turned to Alex. "So whoever wrote that note dismissing me, probably wrote the note to Christina to meet with me".

"Exactly what I was thinking, did you recognise the handwriting"? Alex asked, leaning forward.

"I'm afraid not, I just assumed it was Lord Trafford. He never seemed happy about me talking with Christina".

"She's a widow now, too", Melody clarified, looking into his eyes, a glimmer of hope in hers. "I know she'd love to see you again", she spoke shyly, looking from Alex to Jack.

"Would she now, lass", Jack's eyes twinkled at her. "I think I'd like that too".

Sipping her lemonade, Melody listened as Alex filled Jack in about Christina, and Jack spoke of his life and three grown children and grandchildren, his pride in them evident in his voice. "Well, we better be going, Toby will be needing a break". Glancing at his watch, Alex rose from his chair, shaking Jack's hand. "We have your number now, we'll give you a call once we arrange a meeting with Christina".

"Thanks lad, I'll look forward to it", his gruff reply softened by the twinkle in his eyes. Walking over to a shelving unit, he selected a small cactus. "Here, take this lass, you never know you might have green fingers too", he smiled, handing Melody the plant, delicate hot pink flowers adorned the flat green stems.

"It's beautiful, thank you. What type is it"?

"It's an Easter cactus, likes a sunny spot and a drop of water", he winked at her, his old face still handsome, she noted smiling back at him.

"I'll take good care of it", she promised as they headed outside. "Nice meeting you, Jack".

"And you, lass", he grinned, waving them off.

"He seemed nice", Melody praised as they drove away, the cactus in her hands.

"He did, the old charmer", Alex laughed, looking at the cactus. "I think he has a soft spot for you".

"Oh Alex, really! He's just a lonely, kind old man". Alex's low throated chuckle made Melody's lips twitch with laughter. "Oh, you beast", she laughed, thumping his arm in play. Leaning forward, she switched the radio on, selecting a pop station. 'Better in time', by Leona Lewis was playing. She sat back and closed her eyes as the potent lyrics washed over her, she thought of Jack and Christina.

Pulling up outside the cottage and cutting the engine, Alex turned to Melody who was sleeping peacefully, a slight smile on her lips. Brushing a few wayward curls off her face, he leaned in. "We're home, sweetheart", his breath warming her as her lashes fluttered open, a contented sigh escaping her lips.

"We are", she murmured, straightening up and looking around to get her bearings.

Unclipping his seatbelt, Alex headed around to the passenger back door and let an enthusiastic Toby out, smiling as he watched him head straight to the gate and cock his leg. "Busting was you mate", he chuckled, turning to help Melody out of the SUV.

Entering the cottage, the enticing smell of the lamb casserole had Toby darting to the kitchen, his nose held high. "Always thinking of your belly, aren't you boy", Melody playfully chastised Toby as they followed him in.

"I'm with him there", Alex groaned appreciatively, lifting the slow cook lid to inspect the casserole.

"Alright, you two. I'll feed you both soon", she laughed, placing the cactus on the windowsill.

Scooting Alex and Toby into the garden and grabbing two bottles of beer from the fridge, Melody made her way to the garden and sat down on the lounger, looking at Alex as he stretched out on one beside her. "Dinner should be ready in about thirty minutes", she explained, handing him a beer.

"Oh Mel, anyone ever tell you, you're an angel, a man could get used to this", he murmured, taking a swig from the bottle.

"Once or twice", she laughed, swinging her legs onto her lounger.

"When will you contact Christina about Jack"? She paused, raising her hand to shade her eyes from the sun as she looked at Toby rolling around on the grass.

"Monday probably, I was thinking of calling her from work, I have a couple of questions to ask her".

"Like what"? A small frown settled on her face.

"Well, I was wondering if she would have any old estate workers' documents or any birthday cards from the guests who attended her party that night, so we can compare them to the notes' handwriting".

"But didn't we give them back to her with the journal"?

"I have photocopies of them back at the office", he grinned sheepishly.

"Wouldn't it be perfect if we could get them back together after all these years", Melody dreamily reflected.

"Always the romantic, sweetheart", Alex murmured, gazing appreciatively at her. "How about a little of that directed my way", he teased, opening his arms to her. "Room for two", he patted the lounger as Melody settled down beside him, laying her head on his chest, her head nestled under his chin, her legs entwined with his. Life could not get any better, she mused laying her hand on Alex's chest.

"So, what did you have in mind, a candlelight meal, and flowers"? Feeling his chest rumble with laughter at her words, she inched closer. "Maybe I could spout some poetry", she teased playfully.

He loved the way she always had a smart quip to say, he never knew what to expect from her mouth. Gazing down at her laying stretched out against him, her long bare legs entwined with his, he felt his body tense; she was undoubtedly the complete package. Feelings he had long thought buried bubbling to the surface, placing a finger under her chin, he raised her face to his.

"Shall I compare thee to a summer's day"? He quoted his eyes twinkling playfully as he gazed into her eyes.

"Shakespeare huh, I never imagined you'd know that".

"Ah yes, from my school days, Mrs Cartwright, our old English teacher drummed it into all of us wayward boys", he paused drawing in his breath, "good boys should always learn the sonnets, now turn to sonnet 18 and repeat after me", he mimicked the teacher's high-pitched voice.

"So, you were a wayward boy, were you"? She emphasized the word were playfully, tracing her finger over his lips.

Capturing her finger in his mouth, he had a devilish glint in his eyes. "Still am", he murmured, nipping enticingly at her finger.

Toby's low whine brought their embrace to an end, his nose gently pushing into Melody's thigh. "I think he's telling us it's time for dinner", Melody sighed reluctantly, pushing herself up from the lounger.

"Damn the dog's timing", Alex playfully growled, reaching for the empty beer bottles. "I think we need to set up some boundaries, boy", he playfully chastised Toby as they all headed into the kitchen. Dinner was a success, Melody thought happily as she cleared the plates away while Alex helped himself to another portion of the peach cobbler.

"I better keep an eye on you", she teased, eyeing Alex's second dessert helping.

"My compliments to the chef, another extra mile on my run tomorrow should pay for this", he laughed, tapping his flat stomach.

Melody gazed at him beneath her lashes as he sat at the kitchen table, not for the first time admiring his athletic frame and well-defined muscles. Not an ounce of fat to be seen, the muscles in his strong arms flexing as he spooned the dessert to his mouth, and what a mouth, full and firm lips that had taken her on a sensual journey earlier. She absentmindedly touched her own lips, still swollen from the kisses they had shared. The shrill ring from the telephone pulled Melody from her thoughts, heading quickly into the front room, she answered the call, returning to the kitchen a little while later, a worried frown on her face.

"Problem, love", Alex's concerned voice stopped her mid step.

"That was Sarah", she sighed, "she was just checking up on me. I told her about your offer to investigate Richard". Wringing her hands, she sat down next to Alex.

"And how did she take it"?

"Well, at first she absolutely refused, but after pointing out that it would be better to know one way or the other, she finally accepted".

"And", Alex pressed.

"It's just if we do prove he's cheating, she'll be devastated. I don't know how well she will cope".

"She's stronger than you think love, and she will have you to support her. Who knows it, maybe he's not even playing away".

"Oh, I do hope so". Lifting her head, she gazed at Alex, her tears threatening to spill. "What will you do now"? She asked bravely, blinking the tears away.

"I'll phone Joel tomorrow and set things in motion, and Mel", he paused reaching for her hand, "it'll be okay, try not to worry too much". Staring down at her small hands engulfed in Alex's large ones, she had a comforting feeling that everything would be okay.

Chapter 9

The days flew by as Melody concentrated on her work and making her gown perfect for the upcoming gala. Alex had made good on his promise to get someone onto Richard's case, and soon they would all have an answer. For the millionth time, Melody desperately hoped it would be favourable news.

"What's with the frown, love", Susie's concerned voice pulled Melody from her melancholy thoughts.

"Just thinking of the gala". Melody balked at the little white lie, but it was not her place to talk of Sarah's situation, even though Susie was her dearest friend, whom she would normally confide everything in.

"Ah love, you'll be fine, you have that big strapping fellow Alex to keep you safe", she clucked, shaking her head, a smile playing on her lips. "A fine man, and he really cares about you too". Picking up some papers from the counter, Melody busied herself, shuffling them, aware of Susie's watchful eyes on her. "So how's the gown coming on".

"Oh, it's nearly done. I had it dry cleaned before attaching the lace. I never realised how dusty it was, the rose pink is much prettier than I first realised". Thankful for the change of subject, Melody smiled.

"Sounds lovely, you'll have to show me sometime".

Reaching for her mobile phone, Melody grinned. "I can do one better, I have a picture of it on here". Scrolling through, she found it and handed the phone to Susie.

"Oh wow, it truly is stunning", Susie sighed appreciatively, "you really will be the bell of the ball", her eyes misting as she looked at Melody. "I bet Alex will look good and yummy, all scrubbed up in a tux", she teased as Melody blushed.

"Oh Suse, I'll tell him you said that".

"Well, if you ever get tired of him send him my way, I could teach him a thing or two", she laughed, her mischievous eyes dancing in merriment as she wandered away.

Alex looked at the untouched pile of paperwork on his desk. With only nine days left until the gala, his time that morning had been spent busily checking and double checking the security. Throwing his pen down, he grabbed the top folder, his eyes narrowing as the photos spilled out onto the desk. Damn, he swore as he looked at pictures of Richard and a rather plump blonde girl kissing and holding hands, another of them gazing lovingly into each other's eyes and the most damning as they headed into an apartment building, Richard's hand planted intimately on her backside, no mistaking an illicit relationship. "Damn the man", he growled, slamming his fist on the desk. How was he going to break this news to Melody. He hated the thought of distressing her and her sister, but there was no backing out now they had caught the scumbag red handed.

Taking his wallet out, he opened it to look at the photo he had of Melody tucked inside, her sweet smile warming his heart. If only he had better news for her, he thought, rubbing his finger over her image as if willing her to appear. The business card slotted beside catching his eye, frowning, he pulled it out. 'A1 Employment Agency', he read, suddenly remembering Melody giving it to him, thinking it was his. Pressing his intercom, he waited for his receptionist to answer.

"Yes boss", she quickly responded.

"Jane, is Joel in", he asked, reigning in the impatience in his voice.

"He sure is, want me to send him in".

"That would be great, thanks".

Joel strode into the office minutes later, slumping down in the seat opposite Alex. "You summoned me", he stated, raising an eyebrow at Alex.

"Ah Joel, good to see you. Yes, I wanted to know if this business card belongs to you"? Alex indicated the business card lying on the table.

Joel picked up the card. "Nope, not guilty. Why, do you think I'm looking for er", he paused, taking a closer look "casual work at this A1 Agency".

"No, of course not, it's just that I promised Melody I would ask if it belonged to you".

"And why, prey tell, would she think it's mine". He leaned forward, resting his elbows on the desk, a puzzled look on his face.

"She found it in her front room under the armchair and she knows it's not hers, or any of her friends', or mine", he concluded, frowning.

"So, if it doesn't belong to any of us", Joel paused, leaping up from his chair, "damn, you think it belongs to the thief, don't you"?

"That was my next conclusion", Alex nodded, his expression thoughtful.

"Well, the bugger's finally slipped up, so how do you want to play this out", Joel snapped, dropping the card onto the table. "Guess it's too late for checking for fingerprints", he groaned as he paced up and down, thumping his fist into his hand.

"I was going to see if Frank could pull any from it, it's a long shot but worth a try. Meanwhile, I think I might pay a visit to the agency, see what I can dig up".

Joel nodded at Alex's plan. "Anything I can do, just ask".

"There is one thing you could do for me".

Joel stopped pacing and rested his hands on the back of the chair, looking intently at Alex. "Yes, name it".

"Have you got any plans for Saturday"?

"Nothing important that can't be moved, what do you want me to do, a stakeout"?

Alex laughed at his friend's eagerness. "Nothing like that, actually I want you to come to dinner at Mel's. I have to give her some bad news tonight and I thought a few friends over for dinner on Saturday would cheer her up".

"You got the file on Richard then", Joel stated, his eyes settling on the file on the desk.

"Yes, and it's not good news, I'm afraid".

"Right then, Saturday it is. What time do you want me"?

"Seven, and Joel, be on your best behaviour, I'm inviting Charlotte and Lindsey too". Joel's feigned look of hurt causing Alex to laugh. "You know what I mean, just be your charming self".

"No frisking the pixie, then", Joel grinned at Alex's shocked face. "You know Charlotte, she kind of reminds me of an angry pixie".

"Well then, yes, no frisking pixies, angry or otherwise", Alex laughingly chastised him. Bowing theatrically, Joel left Alex's office.

After placing the two calls to Charlotte and Lindsey, arranging for them to come to the dinner party on Saturday, he sat back in his chair thoughtfully rubbing his chin. Picking up the business card with a tissue to avoid further fingerprints, he jotted down the address carefully, wrapping the card into the tissue and placing it inside his jacket pocket. Dropping it into Frank at the station would be his best course of action and then a visit to the A1 agency. Better to go in person, he theorized that way he could see the honest reaction on their faces as he put his questions to them, something an impersonal phone call could never do.

Stopping by Jane's desk on the way out, he informed her. "I'll be stepping out of the office for a while, if anyone needs me you know what to do".

"Yes boss, and boss", she peered up at him over her glasses.

"Yes".

"Rick came in earlier and left this for you", she waved a manila envelope at him.

"Thanks Jane". Taking the envelope, he headed out of the building.

After calling in to see Detective Frank at the station, and a brief discussion on the business card, he left with Frank's words of caution running through his mind that while he would get the lab to run a fingerprint check on the card, chances were, with all of them touching it, the results may not be good.

"Rooky mistake, Alex", he chastised himself as he headed into the 'coffee pot café'. After ordering an espresso, he made his way to the back of the café. Selecting a secluded booth, he slipped in, placing his cup down and pulling the manila folder from his jacket pocket, unfolding it, he shook the contents free. One photo, a pen drive and a note fell out, the grainy photo taken from a security camera of a small white van, its occupant a slim built Caucasian male, his baseball cap pulled down low on his head, making his face impossible to see. Grabbing the note, he started to read.

'Hey boss, thought you'd better see this. I went to all the local shops with cameras and searched through all the security footage as you asked looking for white vans. It wasn't till I went back to footage from the 12th May, that this popped up. It's from Wilsons Builders Merchant, located opposite the back entrance to Melody's shop. The juicy bit is it seems to be following Melody as her car turns into the entrance, he parks, waits

a bit, then heads over and out of shot. You never get to see his face, but I'd bet my last pound it's our guy. He returns empty handed fifteen minutes later, looking like he's rushing some-where. Check out the pen drive, I copied the clip onto it' Rick.

Alex eyed the photo still again, taking a large swallow of his cooling espresso. If this was their thief, then the net just got a little tighter. "I'm coming for you", he promised, slipping the photo into his pocket and the rest of the contents back into the envelope and inside his jacket. Downing the last of his coffee, he wandered over to the counter, ordering two flat whites to go and a couple of cinnamon buns. He headed out with them and over to Melody's shop.

Susie looked up from her seat at the counter as the bell above the door tinkled, her pricing gun poised in her hand.

"Hi Susie, I bring gifts", Alex greeted her, wiggling the pastry bag in the air.

"Be still my beating heart", she laughed, placing a hand dramatically on her chest, "a good-looking man and pas-tries, can a girl ask for more".

Placing the pastries down, he handed her a coffee. "Flat white two sugars", he confirmed, scanning the shop.

"She's in the back, checking stock", Susie grinned, a knowing look in her eyes.

"You got me", he lifted his hands in playful surrender as he walked to the back room.

He found Melody sitting on a stool at a workbench in the corner of the room hunched over a box, a look of determination etched on her face as she furiously scribbled things down in a notebook beside her.

"Working hard", at his words, Melody snapped her head up, emotions playing across her face, confusion followed quickly with delight.

"Alex, what are you doing here"?

"I brought coffee", he offered handing her the paper cup.

"Oh, I needed this", she smiled, sipping the coffee.

"I left cinnamon buns with Susie, best get one quick if I was you".

"You stop that now mister, only I get to tease Susie about her sweet tooth around here".

"You know, with your hands on your hips like that, you really look quite adorable", his voice husky as he brushed his thumb over her cheek, leaning in to place a kiss there.

"Actually though, I do have a reason for dropping in to see you". He reached into his pocket, pulling out the photo still and handing it to her. "Do you recognise this".

She scanned the photo, a frown appearing on her face. "It's the white van that I thought was following me", she whispered, turning worried eyes to Alex. "How did you get it", she whispered, breathlessly pulling open the workbench draw and retrieving a large magnifying glass.

"It's from Wilsons security footage", he said, leaning in to look at it with her.

Holding the magnifying glass over the photo, she peered at the man. "His face is hidden", disappointment reflected in her voice.

"I know, but it's a start and…"

"Alex, look", Melody interrupted him, excitedly grabbing his arm. "The logo on his baseball cap, I've seen it before, I'm sure". Looking closely at the logo, the bright green letters OJM staggered vertically across the black cap, a silhouette of a man hammering at the letter J only just visible.

"Do you remember where you've seen it".

"No, but it looks familiar", she sighed, resignedly handing it back to him.

"Not to worry sweetheart, I'm sure we'll figure it out", he soothed, slipping it back in his pocket.

"On another issue", he looked down at her, catching her chin in his hand and raising her face to look into her eyes. "I've invited a couple of friends over for dinner Saturday".

"You have? Who"?

"Charlotte, Lindsey and Joel, thought we could make a night of it, you know good food, wine and good company".

"Oh Alex, that sounds lovely, but have you told Charlotte that Joel will be there"?

"No, I thought it better to just surprise her".

"There might be fireworks then", she grinned up at him.

"Not quite the entertainment I was going for, but I've warned Joel to be on his best behaviour", he chuckled, releasing her chin and reluctantly stepping back. "I better go and let you get back to work, I've got to call back round to Frank with this", he tapped his pocket with the photo, "and don't let that go cold". He nodded towards the coffee sitting on the workbench.

Grabbing it, she took a sip. "Thanks Alex", she smiled, watching him leave.

As he reached the door, he swung round and hurriedly retraced his steps back to her. "One more thing, Mel". Plucking the coffee cup from her fingers and placing it on the workbench, he pulled her to her feet, bending his head down, his lips brushing against hers softly at first, deepening as he felt her respond to him, the heat of his body pressing into her. A sigh escaped her as she hungrily leaned into him, the warm smell of his aftershave and skin mingling sensually as she wound her arms around his neck. The sound of Susie's voice in the shop made Melody self-consciously pull back.

"Stay safe", his husky words barely a whisper, as he rested his forehead on hers, trying to calm his ragged breathing. Stepping back, he smiled at the sight of her swollen full lips. "See you tonight, minx", he winked, leaving her standing in the middle of the room, a far off look in her eyes. The taste of his lips lingered on hers, long after he had left the shop.

"There you are! I was going to send a search party for you soon", Susie teased as Melody emerged from the back room, making her way over to the counter and dropping the empty coffee cup in the bin behind it.

"Sorry Suse, got a bit distracted", she sheepishly smiled, crouching down to fuss Toby.

"Casanova brought us cinnamon buns, I've had mine", Susie beamed, patting her stomach in satisfaction. "So, is everything okay, he seemed quite distracted as he left".

"He had a photo to show me, it was of the white van that we think has been following me". Standing up, Melody headed to the computer on the countertop, typing in the letters OJM in the search bar, scrolling through the results but nothing of interest came up.

"So what are you looking for"? Susie asked, looking over Melody's shoulder.

"The man in the van was wearing a baseball cap with these letters on it", she sighed, pointing at the screen. "I thought I might find something on the web, but I'm just getting music bands and science stuff".

"OJM", Susie mused aloud, tapping her mouth thoughtfully, "was there anything else on the cap".

"Just a silhouette of a man hammering at the letter J".

Grabbing her phone, Susie excitedly placed a call. "Hi hun, yes, yes, I'm fine. Just a quick question really, do you remember the name of the company we got to tidy up the garden last summer, is their card still pinned on the fridge? It is, and is there a man hammering the letter J? I see". She turned to Melody, her eyes large and excited, motioning to her for a pen. "No, just finding out for a friend. So what's the number, okay hun, got it. Yes I will, see you later, love you too, bye". Grabbing Melody's hands, she gleefully handed the number to her, repeating her conversation with her husband. "Odd Job Man, we hired them last summer to tidy the garden. If I recall correctly, it's a small company, they hire casual workers over the summer, doing all kinds of odd jobs from gardening to painting and the like".

Melody squeezed Susie's hands. "Oh Susie, you're a star. I'll let Alex know, it could be the lead we're looking for". Finishing the call to Alex, she turned to Susie who was busily re-arranging paper flowers on the counter. "He agrees with me Suse, you're a star, he says the cinnamon buns are on him for the next few weeks".

"Oh my, that man just keeps getting better and better", she laughed, a rather pleased look on her face, "glad to help, just as long as we can pin that nasty rat down, that's all the thanks I need".

Arriving home, Melody felt a lightness in her step as she made her way into the cottage, her full bag of groceries not even slowing her down. The day had flown by with the mood in the shop optimistic and happy. Susie had been on fire with her quick wit and sharp sense of humour, making Melody laugh till her sides hurt, the troubles of the thief and the ensuing situation all but forgotten.

Pouring out a bowl of kibble for Toby and emptying the shopping bag, she set aside the ingredients for the spaghetti bolognaise dinner she had decided to cook for Alex and herself. As she sang along to the radio, thoughts of Alex kissing her earlier played in her mind. Unwrapping the cellophane around the bright yellow chrysanthemums and placing them in a vase on the kitchen table, she stood back admiring them. "Not bad, aye Tob's", she grinned at his dis-interested gaze. "Well, I think they're great, brings a little sunshine inside", she mused as she started busily cooking the dinner.

Later, as she called Sarah, her light mood still reflected in her voice as they chatted, catching up on all their news. Arranging to meet up with her for coffee the following day, the only blight on an otherwise light-hearted chat was when the subject of Richard had come up. Replacing the phone and standing up from the armchair, she felt her mood drop at the memory of Sarah's timid voice asking vague questions about Richard's case, almost as if she did not really want to know. "No news yet", she had hesitantly answered her sister, a feeling of hopelessness enveloping her. Making a mental note to speak to Alex about it later that evening, she made her way back to the kitchen. After checking that the bolognaise was doing well, she replaced the lid and switched off the gas. A deep soak in a bubble bath was just what she needed, she thought, wearily heading to the stairs.

Pulling up outside their cottages, Alex cut the engine. Grabbing the file on Richard and the chilled bottle of chardonnay, he headed into his cottage. After a quick shower, he made his way to Melody's, the prospect of telling her about his findings on Richard making him drag his feet. Letting himself in, he made his way to the bureau, tucking the file away inside. He'd tell her later, he promised himself, returning to the kitchen and pouring two glasses of wine. "Dutch courage", he cynically informed a watchful Toby, taking a large swallow of it, the tones of apple and vanilla tingling on his tongue. Stepping out into the garden with Toby at his heels, he sat on the lounger, his thoughts on Melody. "How will I break it to her, boy", he mused, absent-mindedly rubbing Toby's head.

"There you two are". Melody's cheerful voice snapped him out of his melancholy thoughts. She stood in the doorway, her hair a halo of vibrant gold, falling softly on her shoulders, her skin still pink from the bath. Her aqua t-shirt clinging lovingly to her curves, white shorts showing her beautifully slim long legs, time seemed to stand still as he drank in the sight of her. "One of those for me", she smiled, indicating to the glasses of wine on the table.

"Sure is, sweetheart". Reaching his side, she picked up the glass of wine and sank down onto her lounger. "So any luck with the 'OJM' business enquiries"? She spoke hesitantly, reaching out and patting Toby.

"I called them today, they wouldn't give out any employee information, but they did tell me that they use the A1 Employment Agency, which seems very promising". He paused, taking a sip of wine. "I also paid the A1 Agency a visit today. They took a photocopy of the photo still of the van and I gave them the description of the driver. They promised to get in touch if they could match him with any of their employees, so now it's just a waiting game".

"Well, that sounds good", she smiled, lowering her voice and leaning in closer to him. "I was wondering, have you heard anything on the Richard case"? Averting her eyes and taking a large gulp of her wine, she sat with bated breath.

"Oh yes love, the file came in today". He leaned forward and grasped her hands. "It's not good, I'm afraid", he soothed as her body tensed.

"W-what did you find out".

"I'm sorry Mel, all the evidence points to an affair. We have photos of them together at several locations, I have the file indoors", he revealed.

"Do you know who the woman is"?

"Yes, turns out, she's one of his work colleagues, a claims clerk Alice Parker, do you know her"?

"No, can't say I've heard her name before. Oh god, how am I going to tell Sarah", she cried as the realisation of the whole situation washed over her.

Pulling her over and onto his lap, he rested his chin on the top of her head, gently rocking her. "It's okay, baby", he soothed as she let the stress of the past few days out in silent tears. "You know, Sarah suspected this, at least having it confirmed will help her make the right decisions moving forward", he murmured against her head. Gazing up at him, she sniffed, rubbing the back of her hand across her tear-stained cheeks.

"You're right, she thought she was going crazy with paranoia. At least she will feel some sort of relief now".

"And don't forget she'll have you to help her cope", Alex acknowledged, pulling her tighter in his embrace.

"I think I'll tell her tomorrow when we meet for coffee, it will give me a chance to get it all sorted in my head", she paused, looking towards the back door. "Can you show me the file now"?

"Okay babe, if you think it will help".

"I think I need to know everything Alex", she gulped, stifling fresh tears and standing to go inside, a new determination setting in.

Chapter 10

Tucking her car out of sight in between two large 4x4's, Melody cut the engine, her view to Sarah's drive four houses away just visible. She checked that the file on Richard was still safely stowed away in her tote bag. For what seemed like the millionth time, she went over the evidence in her head, the really damning picture had been of them entering Alice's apartment building, their body language leaving no doubt as to how they intended to finish their evening. Maybe she would only need to show Sarah the photo of their romantic dinner, no need for overkill, she mused, worrying her bottom lip anxiously.

The call to Susie yesterday evening had been quick, letting her know she would be in late to the shop, stating it was a family emergency and reassuring her it was nothing too drastic. She smiled ironically at the thought, "no, just dropping a bombshell and destroying my sister's life". Angrily clenching her fists as the thought of Richard's behaviour over the years bubbled to the surface. As if her thoughts of him had summoned the devil himself, she watched as he placed Lucy in his car, belting her in safely, a smile plastered over his face as he threw his brief case onto the passenger seat and climbed in his car. "Asshole", Melody muttered under her breath, as she waited for him to leave.

She knew he always dropped Lucy to school on a Friday before heading into the office where he worked as an Actuarial Manager for 'Seers Insurance' and today was no different as she watched him pull away.

Butterflies in hobnail boots stamped ferociously in her stomach as she made her way to Sarah's front door and rang the bell. "Did you forget something I…", Sarah's voiced trailed off, her surprise at seeing Melody this early standing on her doorstep stamped clearly on her face. "Mel, what a surprise. I thought we were meeting for coffee at one"?

"This couldn't wait, I'm afraid", she groaned, stepping into the hall.

"It's about Richard, isn't it", Sarah blurted, leaning against the now closed front door.

"I'm afraid so, sis". Grabbing her sister's hand in support and walking her to the front room, they sat down on the large black leather sofa together.

The front room was styled simply with two large alcoves standing on either side of a large fireplace, a few books and photos placed strategically on the shelves, a large mirror reflecting the room's windows hung directly above the ivory-coloured ornate stone mantelpiece, two large ivory pillar candles its only adornment. An oval glass top coffee table sat in the middle of the room, the abstract carved stone base always reminded Melody of a wave rising from the blended cream and blue wavy lined rug. In the far corner, sitting on a marble stand, a huge flat screen television dominated the room, a few of Lucy's DVDs scattered before it as if she had just been there.

"I knew this was coming, I prepared myself and everything, but I'm still not sure I'm ready", Sarah sniffed, tears brimming in her eyes. Grabbing a tissue from the tissue box on the coffee table, she dabbed furiously at her eyes. "Is he having an a-affair", she stuttered, turning to look at Melody.

"Oh hun, I'm so sorry, but yes he is". Reaching out her arms to Sarah, she leant in to hug her.

"Please Mel, no". Putting her hands up to stop Melody's embrace, "I can't be touched right now, I'll fall apart", she gave a watery smile, "I need to hear it all first".

Melody's drive to the shop seemed to take forever as she pondered over her sister's reaction to the news of Richard's infidelity. Her tears had soon given way to anger and her calm resolve to leave him had surprised Melody. She had thought her sister would fall apart, but this new stronger Sarah had blind-sided her. "Things haven't been good between us for years, I've thought about leaving him before, but I've always tried to stay for Lucy's sake", Sarah's words bounced around in her head as she searched her memory for signs that things had not been right for so long, and how she could have not noticed. She felt so guilty. "If you hadn't avoided situations with him, you would have noticed", she berated herself.

Alex had been right. Sarah was made of sterner stuff than she had ever given her credit for. Sarah had insisted on seeing all the files, including the incriminating photos, insisting it was better to have it all out on the table, no hidden surprises. Leaving the file with Sarah at her request had seemed like all she could do in the situation. She just hoped Alex wouldn't mind, he probably had a copy of it anyway, she told herself trying to ease the worry that had settled over her.

After grabbing two coffees, she headed into the shop. Susie's sing-song voice greeted her, "Here she is Toby, and with coffee too". Toby bounded over, greeting Melody like she had been gone for a week.

"Oh Tob's, you maniac", Melody laughed, scratching his head with her free hand.

"Alex dropped him off this morning, thought you might miss him, he said", Susie laughed, eyeing the adoration in Toby's eyes. "I think he missed you more though, every time someone came into the shop, he would get all excited until he realised it wasn't you, didn't you boy". She crooned, waving his purple plushie at him. Eyeing his toy, he rushed over to her and took hold of it; a tug-o-war game ensued till Susie gave in letting him claim his prize.

"So, is everything okay? Did you sort out your family crisis"?

Melody nodded, handing a coffee to Susie. "For now", she muttered, changing the subject. "I'm going to do the stock order today, anything you want to add"? Melody indicated to the clipboard on the counter.

"I've added a couple of things to the list already", Susie beamed, adding, "Casanova kept to his word", pointing to a fresh pastry bag on the counter. "How about we indulge in them with our coffees".

"Sounds good", Melody smiled, glad of the change of mood.

At one o'clock precisely, Sarah entered the shop. Gone was the flowery dress and messy bun, now standing there, dressed in a pin stripped trouser suit, her hair cut into a short bob, one side slightly longer, the thick dark brown bangs streaked with caramel highlights softening the look. "Can I help you miss", Melody greeted as she made her way across the shop floor, her tote bag slung over her shoulder.

"It's me, Mel", Sarah smiled at her shocked face, "we did say one o'clock, didn't we".

"Oh, my god! Sarah? You look so different, what's going on"?

Linking arms with her, Sarah ushered them out of the shop and over to the coffee house. Ordering two coffees and selecting a booth, they sat down opposite each other.

"Well, what's with all this", Melody waved her hand at her sister's new look.

"I just decided a change was in order, do you like it"?

"Like it? I love it", Melody enthused, a bemused smile on her face, "but what's with the clothes"?

"I've been to see the solicitors, with the file you gave me. He said the divorce should be plain sailing".

"So you're really doing it then".

"Yes, once I'd made up my mind, I saw no reason to delay. Also, I've got a job interview in an hour".

"Wow sis, you really are moving on, where's the job"?

"It's just for an entry level office assistant at 'Picture Perfect', you know the photography shop just down the road".

"I know it, they did Lucy's birthday photos last year, didn't they"?

"Yep, that's the one. It would be a good job to get me back into the workforce", she sighed, taking a sip of her cappuccino and licking the froth off her top lip.

"I think it's a good idea; you always said you would return to work when Lucy started school, I never understood why you didn't".

"Rich always wanted me to stay at home, said I didn't need to work and I guess I just went with it, but not anymore", she admitted, a determined look on her face.

"What's been happening with you, are you and Alex an item now"? Sarah asked, leaning forward, searching her sister's face.

"We are, but we're taking it slow", she confessed, playing distractedly with her coffee cup.

"That's the best way, I never could understand why people rush into things these days", she sighed, reaching out to squeeze Melody's hand. "How are the plans coming along for the gala"?

"Alex has it all under control, and my gown is finished". Reaching into her bag, she pulled out her phone, scrolling through the photos, she found the latest snap of her gown. "Here it is", passing Sarah the phone to look.

"Oh my, it's beautiful, you will look amazing", she enthused sliding the phone back across the table, "but will you be safe? I haven't seen your bodyguard lately", she stated, peering around the restaurant anxiously.

"Yes, I'll be safe. Alex has his best men working security and of course, he'll be by my side". Taking a sip of her coffee, she continued. "Besides, it's going to be bursting at the seams with guests. I'm sure no-one would try to do anything. And since the newspaper ran that article, I haven't seen the white van. The thief probably knows the necklace is no longer in my possession, so I'm not in any danger sis. As for Rick, he is no longer on duty".

"I can't say I like it, Mel, I just hope you're right". Shifting forward, she smiled. "So tell me sis, what's the latest with Charlotte. Is she still mad over that new guy at the vets"? They spent the next few minutes chatting light-heartedly, the laughter continuing as they headed back over to Melody's shop. "Thanks for this", Sarah sighed, hugging Melody tightly.

"Yes, it's been good for us both", Melody conceded, feeling happier with her sister's new positive outlook. Stepping back, she looked at her. "Now go, knock them dead", she laughed as Sarah shrugged, turning to leave, "and sis, let me know how it goes", she called after her.

"I will", she promised, blowing a kiss at Melody as she walked away.

Alex watched the security surveillance footage playing over on a loop on his computer, glad he had kept the pen drive and let Frank take a copy of it, while he had waited at the station. Pausing the footage at the sight of the van stopping on the road, he clicked it on frame by frame. Alex sat bolt upright in his chair, the frame paused on the man as he stood beside the van zooming in. He leaned in closer, scanning the frame. The sideways shot of the man revealed his baseball cap pulled low on his face, his lank brown jaw length hair hanging untidily around his face. Clicking the frames on until he stopped again as the man crossed the road and stood at the entranceway to the back of the shops. Dressed in scruffy jeans and a grey sweatshirt and what looked like black work boots, he stood watching the back of the shops. "What are you up to"? Alex muttered to himself, he certainly looked like a casual worker, but something did not feel right about him.

Pressing play, he watched as the man stood for a few minutes, his hand clenched tightly by his side, his fingers slowly uncurling as if he was counting. Pausing the frame, he zoomed in on the man's hand, his four fingers held straight down his thumb tucked up in his palm, grabbing the basic map of the shops; Alex counted circling the fourth one in red biro. Pulling up the street view of the shops on google maps, he counted again stopping on the fourth building once again, an outdated shot of 'Simple Crafts' filled the screen. "Got you", he seethed, slamming his fist on the table; this had to be their guy, he was certain of it now.

Pressing play once again, he watched as the man headed towards the front of the shops and out of sight. Rewinding the footage and freezing it as the man turned side-ways to walk to the front of the shops, he zoomed in; he took a screenshot and sent it to the printer. He stared at the screen scribbling notes down; five foot nine or ten, slim build, late forties, scruffy brown jaw length hair, slightly stooped shoulders. Dropping his pen on the desk, he picked up the photo still from the printer; picking up his phone, he made a call. "Rick, Alex here, where are you now? Right, change of plans mate; I want you back on bodyguard duty for Melody, thing is this time I want you to keep your distance. Yes, alright I see, but I don't want her to know, no point worrying her again". Briefing him on the footage of him counting the shops and the rough description of the man, he ended the call. Time to press the agency again, he decided; grabbing the photo still and his notes, he headed out of the office.

"Can I help you sir"? A girl dressed in a navy suit with a name badge pinned on her jacket lapel enquired as he stood waiting in the A1 Employment Agency; he quickly made his way over to her, checking her name badge. "Hi Sandra", he spoke, flashing his best charming smile at her. "I'm here to see a Mrs Harper".

"Do you have an appointment", she blushed making her way back around her desk to the open diary. He guessed she was new at this job, she was at best only eighteen years old, her hesitancy spoke volumes to him, and he was sure she had not been here last time he had called into the Agency.

Alex watched as she fussed over the diary, her long red painted nails tapping the pages, her brown hair held back in a low ponytail hung over her shoulder. "No, I don't have an appointment, but I need to speak with her today". The refusal dying on her lips as he leaned over the desk giving her his lop-sided smile. "But it is quite important, and it will only take a few minutes" he coaxed.

"Okay, I'll see if she can fit you in Mr…"?

"Knight, Alex Knight".

Watching as Sandra hurried towards the back of the building and disappeared into one of the doors, Alex sank into a seat opposite her desk. The small room seemed crammed full, with four desks lining each wall, most of them currently occupied with employees busily typing away on their computers. A pathway between the rows of desks leading to what he assumed were two back offices, both with their doors shut, one being Mrs Harper's he guessed as that had been the door Sandra had disappeared into, and to the right of them, another room, its door wide open revealing it to be a stock room full of boxes and office paraphernalia. A large photocopier stood to one side, which was currently spouting out photocopies while a flustered looking middle-aged woman with a pencil wedged into her neat bun styled hair, busily collected them and meticulously shuffled the copies into order.

Posters of different jobs lined the walls from gardening to office work, each with a catchy slogan, 'we cater for all, so give us a call'. One poster boasted, a picture of a man and woman, each balancing a tray dressed in black and white service uniforms. Looking at the cork board behind Sandra's desk, he scanned the advertisements and holiday postcards dotted all over it, with a few witty pictures peeking through them, one caught his eye, it was of a toothbrush, the words 'I do the worst job'! Bubbling out of it, next to it a toilet plunger, its bubble stating 'really'? The corny picture making his lips twitch in amusement.

"She will see you now", Sandra's timid voice pulled him from his musings. "Door number 1", she pointed towards the back.

"Thanks", he smiled, making his way to the back, a determination in his stride. Closing the door behind him, he walked over to the desk.

"Take a seat Mr Knight", she indicated to the chair opposite her desk. "Now how may I help you", she asked, peering over her glasses at him. With steel grey hair pinned into a severe bun, the half-moon glasses perched precariously on the end of her nose, a beaded glasses chain hanging on each side of her face, her crisp white blouse continued the look of severity tucked into a navy pencil skirt, the matching jacket hanging on the back of her chair, she reminded Alex of a school matron, momentarily silencing him.

"Well", she prodded, arching a well plucked eyebrow at him.

"I was hoping you might have some information for me", he smiled, gathering his wits about him and reaching into his jacket pocket, withdrawing the photo still. "I came in the other day with another photo of this guy", he pointed to the photo handing it over to her, "another lady I spoke to that day said you may employ him, I was hoping you may recognise him".

Pushing her glasses up, she peered at the photo shaking her head. "We employ a multitude of people Mr Knight, and this is a rather vague photo, and even if I could recognise him, I'm sure you're aware that we are not in the habit of divulging employee's personal details", she reproached, handing him back the photo in a dismissive manner.

"I'm well aware of that, but Mrs Harper, this person may be responsible for a break-in and following a young woman. We need to rule him out, the police already have this companies' business card that we believe the thief dropped at the crime scene, so they may be in asking you these very same questions", he appealed, handing her the photo once again.

Sighing, she reluctantly studied the photo, a frown settling on her face. "He was wearing an 'odd job man' baseball cap, whom I happen to know you find workers for", Alex pressed, as she made her way over to a filing cabinet.

Returning to sit with two thin files, "Okay Mr Knight, one of these may or may not be your man", she conceded, opening the top file, "do you have any other helpful information that might match one of these men to yours", she paused tapping the files.

"He's approximately late forties, approximately five foot nine or ten, drives an old model white ford transit connect van, brown jaw length hair", he paused as she closed the first file, flipping the second one open and running her finger over the contents.

Pausing, she tapped her finger on one line, "this could be a match", she looked up from the file "now as I said, I can't give out too much information", she peered over her glasses at him continuing, "this client is forty-eight and drives a white transit van, he has indeed worked for OJM, and matches the description you've provided". Steepling her fingers, she leaned forward on her elbows, eyeing Alex intently. "If I do provide you with his name, you must promise to never divulge to anyone that it was from us, it could cause all kinds of trouble".

"I understand, you have my word, when I speak to detective Marsh, I won't reveal your company as my source". Grabbing a scrap of paper, she wrote down the name, holding it out to him.

"I hope you catch him if he really is responsible for the break-in, my husband and I got broken into last year, I've never felt the same since", she confessed, a sad smile softening her face.

"Thank you Mrs Harper this is great". Alex stood, picking up the photo still from the desk and slipping it into his jacket pocket. Pausing, he looked at her, reaching behind, he retrieved his wallet from his back pocket and pulled out his business card. "If you ever need any security installed just give me a call", he smiled, handing the card to her.

"I'm sure that won't be necessary, but thank you Mr Knight". She stood, taking the card and shaking his hand.

Standing outside the agency, he glanced down at the piece of paper and the name scrawled across the page. "Well Tim Abbott, I'm coming for you", he snarled, stuffing the paper in his trouser pocket as he strode purposefully towards his office.

Chapter 11

Having dropped Toby home after work an hour ago, Melody now made her way to her car, her shopping bags weighing heavily in her hands with all the groceries she had bought for the up-coming dinner party on Saturday. She could probably feed an army, she grimaced as she shifted the biting handles to a slightly more comfortable position and hitching her tote bag higher on her shoulder. Locating her car in the busy supermarket car park, she loaded the shopping bags into the back seat, sliding into the driver's seat, she threw her bag onto the passenger side. A large glass of wine is just what she needed now, she mused, turning the key in the ignition. The car started, spluttered and choked; turning the key again, she tried to start the car but the engine just made a coughing sound refusing to turn over. "Damn", she swore, resting her head on the steering wheel, a brisk knock on her window making her start. Standing, peering in at her, stood Richard, a half-smile on his face. Winding the window down, she thanked her lucky stars the electrics of the car still worked.

"Bit of car trouble, Mel"? He leaned in, a smug smile settling on his face.

"Err yes, what are you doing here", she snapped, thinking how could this day get any worse.

"Shopping of course", he lifted a small bag of groceries, "let me give you a lift, you can call a tow company from my car if you like".

Bristling, she refused, adding, "it's okay, I'll just call a cab".

"Aw come-on Mel, that will take ages and your shopping will spoil", he glanced at the bags in the back, "besides I pass your way on my way home". Dropping her hands into her lap, Melody chewed on her bottom lip, she had so much left to do at home, she didn't really have the time for this latest crisis. Surely accepting a lift from Richard wouldn't be too bad; besides, he was right, by the time a cab would arrive, her groceries would spoil.

"Well, if you're sure", she smiled tightly, reaching for her bag and closing the window, stepping out of the car as he grabbed her grocery bags from the back.

"Over there", he nodded towards his car, heading off to stow the bags in his boot. After locking her car, she made her way over to him, reluctantly sliding into the passenger seat.

"What do you mean, you lost her"! Alex growled down the phone as Rick explained again how he had found her car abandoned in the supermarket car park.

"One minute she was loading groceries into her car, next minute she was gone", he groaned, "a bloody minivan blocked my view for like two minutes I swear".

"Check the supermarket, maybe she went back in for something, and Rick, call me immediately if you find her". Alex hung up, grabbing his jacket, he ran from the office and past a startled Jane to his car, maybe she headed home with a friend, he desperately thought instantly rejecting the idea. Dialling her number, he reached her voicemail again. "Damn", he swore, raking his hand through his hair, "where are you, Mel"?

Richard drove them out of the supermarket car park, the silence between them grating on his nerves. Casting a look at her, he felt his anger boil; sitting back, resting her head on the headrest, her eyes closed like nothing was amiss, a carefree smile on her face. Well he would show that prissy little bitch, he thought, a malevolent look in his eyes. Turning back to the road, he took a turning towards an abandoned industrial estate, stopping the car, a short while later at the back of one of the derelict old buildings, he cut the engine.

"W-where the hell are we"? Melody stuttered glancing around at the unfamiliar sight, a frisson of fear enveloping her.

"Now, now, where are your manners? Is our princess finally awake", he sneered, a look of pure evil on his face.

"Richard, what's going on"? She begged, pulling in vain at the car door handle.

"I'm afraid not, child locks come in very handy", he cruelly laughed as she looked wildly around for escape, his hand snaking out and resting on her knee.

"Get off me, you scumbag", she grated out, flicking his hand away.

"That's no way to talk to your dear brother-in-law", he snarled, "you always thought you were better than me, didn't you princess"?

"Please Richard, I don't know why you're doing this but just stop it and take me home", she pleaded looking at him, his face now contorted with rage, making him look like a stranger to her.

"Little innocent Melody, claiming she knows nothing. Well, it was your boyfriend who you had follow me, wasn't it, getting some good snaps of me with another woman trying to wreck my marriage, or do you still want to play clueless"? He mocked leaning into her, his warm breath on her face making her stomach turn. "Meddling in things that don't concern you, have consequences princess".

"But you are cheating on my sister", she gasped, reeling from the venom dripping in his voice.

"Yes and everything was fine until you decided to stick your nose in and mess things up, now she's talking about divorcing me"!

"You vile creep! You have never been good enough for my sister, always wanting things you can't have. Well, now she has finally seen you for the cheating pig you really are", she ranted, her anger driving her on. "I'm glad she's divorcing you".

Pain exploded on her face, her head snapping back as his hand connected with her cheek. "Bitch", he growled, lurching for her, grabbing her hair painfully as he dragged her forward sinking his head to hers, his wet mouth roughly kissing her, his other hand groping at her blouse. "Come on darling, show me some love, I don't mind it a bit rough", he jeered as she fought desperately against him. Melody pushed at his chest as he pressed against her, her mind racing; she must find a way out, this could not be happening to her, she thought as wave after wave of sickness surged through her, the smell of Richard's cloying cologne assailing her nostrils.

The sound of her blouse ripping making him pause, a leery look on his face before he sank down once again, ravaging her lips. Not knowing if the taste of blood in her mouth was his or hers as she fought the over-whelming dizziness threatening her, closing her eyes to gather strength for one last fight, she must not faint, she thought desperately somehow, she had to stop this craziness. Suddenly his weight lifted from her, and she heard a crunch. Opening her eyes, she saw him lying on the ground outside of the car nursing his jaw, two men towering over him. She could not see the men's faces, just their jean clad legs, watching as if locked in a trance as one pair of the legs disappeared from sight, her feeling of relief only temporary as the car door behind her back opened and she was pulled into strong arms. Bracing herself for a fight, she kicked out wildly. "Stop Mel, it's me", Alex spun her around, gently pulling her blouse together, "it's okay, I've got you", he soothed, the look of relief stamped all over his face.

Turning, they watched as Rick hauled a now whimpering Richard up off the floor, cuffing his hands behind his back and shoving him into his waiting truck. "Okay boss, I'll take him in to the cops, you follow on behind", he signalled to his truck as he turned to walk away.

"H-how did you find me"? She stuttered, turning back to Alex, a bemused look on her face.

"I set up a find my phone app on your phone", he murmured, stroking his knuckles over her face, "when Rick found your car abandoned and you didn't answer my calls, I activated it".

"The car, it broke down, I only accepted his offer of a lift, I thought he was going to…", she stopped, her voice trailing as a sob broke out.

"Shh, it's okay, don't think about it sweetheart", his voice was soft, not betraying the pent up anger he could barely keep inside. Grabbing her tote bag, he handed it to her and led her to his SUV and settled her in. "We have to go to the cops now". Catching the look of panic in her eyes, he added quietly. "You need to give a statement, shouldn't be too bad".

"My groceries", she hiccupped, glancing towards Richard's car.

"I'll get them, you wait here", he smiled shutting the door.

The drive home was quick, the normality of Alex's easy chat about the traffic and light-hearted topics soothing her frayed nerves. The statement to the female officer in the comfort suite had been bearable in the circumstances. Answering the questions of who, when and where it had happened and giving her detailed statement left her shaken; the fact that he was now in custody and would be arrested for assault, of little comfort to her as she worried about the repercussions it would have on her sister.

Having her bruises photographed and her mouth swabbed, had felt more than intrusive. Alex had luckily produced a spare t-shirt he had stowed away in his SUV, as if he had already known it would be needed. Handing it to her as she entered the comfort suite, the realisation of why he had given it to her when the female officer asked for her to remove her torn blouse for evidence.

Sitting there now in his over-sized t-shirt she glanced at him; he had been a rock for her, his insistence that she report Richard straight away, while it was still fresh in her mind had been for the best. He had handled everything for her, even producing a coffee while she waited for the female officer to check on the situation outside the room. When the officer returned with pamphlets, he stayed as she updated them on Richard's arrest, the details of what would happen next, when a court date would most likely be set and promising to keep her informed. Alex had been there, taking it all in, holding her hand and encouraging her, letting her know she was not alone. Quickly escorting her back to his SUV and out of the police station, how she would have managed it all without him, she shuddered to think.

Pulling up outside her cottage, he helped her out of the SUV, grabbing the groceries and walking her inside, all the while keeping a firm hand on her elbow to steady her. "I think I'll go have a quick shower", she sighed, looking down at his t-shirt she wore.

"Okay sweetheart, I'll be down here making a few calls, fancy a glass of wine when you come down"?

"Yes please, and Alex", she paused, looking at him, his eyes cloudy with an emotion she couldn't quite read, "thank you, again", she turned to the stairs and slowly made her way up.

Standing under the powerful shower, Melody scrubbed at her skin until it was pink and stinging, the feel of Richard's groping hands still on her body, making her scrub harder. Bewildered thoughts running rampantly through her head, what was Richard thinking? Why would he do this to her? Would he have gone any further? "Stop it now", she moaned aloud to herself, refusing to let her mind wander down that avenue of thought. Cutting the water, she stepped out of the shower, wrapping a towel around herself as she wandered to her room, the familiar surroundings, a balm to her over-active mind. Pulling on tracksuit bottoms and a loose-fitting t-shirt, she slipped her feet into her slippers and sat down at the dressing table. Picking up her comb, she set about untangling her wet hair, the sound of Alex's low rumbling voice below in the kitchen reassuring her. Fingering her swollen split lip, she stared at her reflection, wide frightened eyes stared back, the bruise on her face already turning purple. Moving her fingers tentatively to her collar bone, she gently rubbed at her bruises, now hidden beneath the t-shirt. She shivered, if Alex had not found her... "Stop it Melody", she chastised herself, standing abruptly and heading for the stairs, a glass of wine and Alex's company was what she needed, she told herself as she descended the stairs.

Entering the kitchen, she found Alex busily putting the groceries away, two glasses of wine sat on the kitchen table, along with his phone and a stack of files. "Working"? She implied, fingering the files.

"Nothing that can't wait", he smiled, scooping them up and placing them in his case. "You're looking better", his warm smile reached his eyes as they settled on her.

"Alex", she hesitated, "how did Rick know my car was abandoned"?

"I had him tailing you".

"You did", her eyes were wide with confusion.

"Yes, I'll explain later. Now why don't you take your wine and curl up on the sofa, I'm making you chilli-con-carne for dinner, so you can just sit back and be pampered". She took the wine he held out to her and nodded, too exhausted to question him further.

"You really live up to your name", she half-heartedly teased, a raised eyebrow his questioning response. "My Knight in shining armour", she confirmed, laughing wearily and scooting into the front room to avoid being tickled by him as he made a move to get her, his arms outstretched, his fingers wiggling in a playful tickling motion.

After a dinner of chilli-con-carne and crusty bread rolls, she felt more human, the wine having had a relaxing effect on her. She snuggled into Alex, the sound of Toby snoring peacefully against the sofa making her sleepy.

"I don't want to ever move", she yawned, resting her head on his chest and listening to him breathing.

"Then don't", he whispered, trailing his fingers up and down her arm.

"Have to, I've got to call Sarah to tell her about Rich-ard", she groaned, the inevitable conversation unsettling her.

"I've spoken to her already", he sighed, releasing her as she pulled away to look up at him.

"You have, when"?

"I called her while you were in the shower".

"H-how did she take it"? She stuttered, her eyes wide with worry.

"She was shocked but more than anything, she was concerned about you. I told her you would call her tomorrow when you've rested".

Settling back down against him, she trailed her fingers over his chest, "thank you, I was dreading that call, you really are my Knight aren't you".

"At your service milady", he joked, pulling her deeper into his arms and placing a kiss on the top of her head.

Chapter 12

The morning sunshine streamed in through the curtains as Melody woke, her face and body aching, the memories of the previous day flooded her sleepy mind. Groaning, she glanced at the bedside alarm clock, the red display blinked 7.20 at her. "Too early", she muttered, pulling the duvet over her head, but sleep would not come as her mind re-played the events of yesterday over and over. The knowledge that Alex had re-instated Rick to watch over her puzzled her, she had been too exhausted to question him about it yesterday, but now she wanted answers. Why had he thought she needed Rick, was the thief back? Giving up the hope of more sleep, she gingerly got out of bed; opening her curtains, she peered out, her little red clio parked in its usual place made her frown, how had that got there? She groaned, remembering she had forgotten to call the tow company yesterday. Alex must have taken care of that too, but that was quick. Surely the mechanics would not have had time to fix it, she mused, thanking her lucky stars that she wouldn't be needing it for work that day. Pulling on her robe and checking her mirror, she gazed at her face in dismay, at her unsightly bruises, her swollen cheek and eye now shades of purple and yellow, the cut on her swollen lip red and angry looking. No amount of makeup would disguise them, she winced, running her fingers through her hair; she gave up trying to tidy her appearance and headed for her door.

Creeping down the hallway, listening out for any sounds that Alex might be awake, she made her way to the stairway, the silence of the cottage magnifying the sound of the stairs as they creaked under her slippered feet. Entering the kitchen, she saw his laptop and files splayed over the kitchen table, an empty mug sat rinsed on the draining board. Toby yawned and slowly stretched as he made his way over to her in greeting. "Morning Tob's", she whispered, looking towards the front room and the sofa where Alex had left his pillow and blanket neatly piled at the end.

Disappointed at finding the cottage empty, she turned back into the kitchen, busily pouring Toby some kibble and herself a coffee.

"Morning sweetheart", Alex's gentle greeting from the backdoor stopped her midway from sipping her coffee.

"Morning Alex", she turned, smiling at him, the shock in his eyes at her fresh bruises making her feel self-conscious.

"Oh love", he sighed, striding over to her and cupping her face gently, "it's okay, they'll fade" he murmured dropping feather light kisses on her face.

"I know but meanwhile I look like a monster", she grimaced pulling away.

"You could never look like a monster, sweetheart", the honesty on his face betrayed his emotions, making her relax as he pulled her back into his arms.

"You're all sweaty", she laughed, wrinkling her nose and pulling back, looking him up and down, his damp t-shirt clinging to his broad chest and running shorts revealing his strong tanned muscular thighs.

"Happens when I go running", he smiled, grabbing the lapels of her robe and pulling her back to him.

"Oh, you beast", she playfully admonished. "How about you take the first shower while I fix us some breakfast", she offered, moving over to the fridge. How about we save water and share a shower, he thought, stopping himself just in time from speaking his mind. He watched her bending into the fridge, her long legs revealed in the short robe, better make it a cold shower, he thought, smiling wryly as visions of her sharing his shower sent his pulse racing.

"What"? She asked, looking at the smile playing on his face.

"Just admiring the view", his voice sounding husky.

Placing the eggs and bacon on the counter, she poured them both a coffee. "Here, have this first". She handed the mug to him as he sat at the kitchen table. "I saw my car outside, was it fixed already"?

"It's fixed, turns out it was nothing serious, just a rag stuffed up the exhaust pipe, an old trick to stall a car", his voice barely concealing the anger he felt. Catching his hand in hers as he twined her belt around his fingers, she turned it over examining the back of his hand.

"What's this", she implored, staring at his scuffed knuckles.

"I couldn't help myself Mel, he had it coming".

"Y-you mean Richard"? She stuttered.

"Yes, I hit him the other day, but I'm not sorry. He's lucky that's all I did, if Rick hadn't taken him I…",

"It's okay, I'm kind of glad you did", she reassured him, looking at his face, the distress written all over it. A feeling of protectiveness and love welled up inside her, now where had that come from. Swallowing the feeling and hoping she had not betrayed her thoughts, she pinned a bright smile on her face. "We'll make a right pair if we go out like this", she smiled at the irony of the situation.

"Staying in could be fun", he grinned, wiggling his eyebrows at her playfully.

"Oh no, we have a dinner party tonight", she groaned remembering the friends they had invited.

"We can cancel if you don't feel up to it", he suggested, looking into her eyes.

"No, let's leave it as it is, it will give me something to take my mind off all this", she gestured to her bruised face, "now let me get some ointment and sort out your hand Mr", sashaying away to retrieve her first aid kit, a refusal dying on his lips at her determined attitude.

Dabbing at his knuckles, she glanced up at him beneath her lashes. "So Alex, why did you feel the need to have Rick guarding me again"? He shifted forward in his seat gazing at her, the bruises on her cheek looking so tender. For a fleeting moment, he considered not telling her as she had been through too much already, but as their gazes met, the trust so readily available in her eyes, he found himself telling it all.

"I found out some more information on our thief, and I just had a gut reaction and wanted to keep you safe".

"What did you find out about him", she stopped dabbing at his knuckles and closed the first aid box, a worried frown on her face.

"Security footage confirms that he was following you on the day of the break-in, and after following some leads, I found out his name is Tim Abbott. I've informed detective Marsh, and everything is under control, but I wanted to be sure that he wouldn't follow you again", he paused reaching out for her hand, "and I'm damn glad I did now". Stepping away, she picked up the eggs and bacon, busying herself with preparing the breakfast; she did not know what to say, she didn't even know how she felt about it all, the enormity of it all weighing down on her.

"Better go for that shower now", she sighed, popping the bread in the toaster and turning to him, the turmoil evident in her eyes.

"It will be okay, love", he insisted.

"I know", she shrugged, putting on a brave face, "five minutes", she clarified, smiling at him as she scooted him out of the kitchen. Grabbing his holdall, he reluctantly made his way to the stairs.

Sitting in the garden dressed in shell pink shorts and a matching pink crop top, feeling refreshed after her shower, Melody glanced down at her legs, the tan she was working on deeper now, the sunscreen making them shine in the bright sun. Her book held loosely in her hands, thoughts of yesterday buzzing around in her head, she would have to call Sarah soon, the sound of Alex tapping away on his laptop in the kitchen, a welcome distraction from her worrying thoughts.

Thinking of Alex and analysing her feelings for him took her thoughts in a different direction; did she love him, where had that feeling of protectiveness and love come from earlier? It had crept up on her, one minute she was adamant it was just the shock of everything that was happening to her. 'But is it'? A tiny voice mocked her, you can't get him out of your head, and melting in his arms, the way he so easily sends your pulse racing. "Oh god, I love him". Melody was shaken by the intensity of her newly discovered feelings. Closing her eyes, she laid back on the lounger, discarding her book on the floor. Toby's head resting reassuringly on her thigh, birds chirping in the trees, the sound of Alex typing lulled her to sleep.

Waking to the sound of hushed voices, Melody sat up looking around her; she was alone in the garden, Toby lay beneath the garden table in the shade; the voices coming from the kitchen continued. Swinging her legs off the lounger, she headed into the cottage. Alex and Sarah sat at the kitchen table, their hushed conversation stopping as soon as she walked in.

"Oh my poor love", Sarah gasped, rushing over to her and throwing her arms around her.

"It looks worse than it is", she sighed, feeling relieved at her sister's warmth. She had known that her sister wouldn't blame her but she had felt guilty none the less, had even dreaded seeing her for the first time since it had happened.

"I know I said I'd wait till you called me, but I just had to see you for myself", she explained, stroking her hand gently over the bruises, "I'm so sorry Mel, how could he do this to you"? She cried, the anguish on her face nearly undoing Melody.

"It's not your fault sis, please", she implored, stepping back.

"But it is, if I hadn't told him I was filing for divorce", she sheepishly looked at her and continued, "he told me I'd never get one, so I told him about the photos and that my solicitor said it would be easy and…".

"Stop", Melody held her hand up, halting Sarah's chatter, "no-ones to blame but him, he did this, not you not me, he cheated on you, then assaulted me, he's the only one who's to blame".

Sarah stood motionless, her shoulders drooping. "I know, and it's such a mess, I just wish I hadn't said anything about the damn photos."

"He pushes my buttons every time", draping her arm over her sister's shoulders, Melody led her to the front room, shooting a look at Alex as he motioned the sign for a cuppa; she nodded in acceptance, mouthing a silent 'thank you' and walked them over to the sofa.

Alex hurried around the kitchen, collecting mugs, now where had she put the t-bags. Pulling open cupboards in search of them, his usual calm demeanour deserting him, the call to Marsh still playing on his mind, no records of a Tim Abbott could be found, the man was a ghost. "Well, I just became a ghost hunter", his frustration making him slam the cupboard door a little harder than it warranted.

"Everything okay in there"? Mel's concerned voice filtered through.

"Just looking for teabags".

"Top right-hand cupboard beside the cooker".

"Thanks". Get it together Alex, he silently berated himself, plopping teabags into the cups and adding hot water.

Seeing Mel all bruised and fragile had nearly sent him over the edge; he had wanted to keep her safe and had failed, damn it he had failed terribly. The new feelings he felt for her crashed over him once again, he had known he cared deeply for her, but lying on the sofa last night, stronger feelings had started to intrude on his overly tired mind. The thought of her lying just above him, tucked up safely in her bed had haunted him, a yearning to hold her, overwhelming his common sense, making him walk to the stairs several times that night, only to return to the sofa as he thought better of it. His declaration of love was probably the last thing she needed right then; love, the word so readily formed in his head, did he love her. 'If it looks like a duck', he quoted aloud, a saying Joel always produced whenever stating the obvious.

"Walks like a duck, probably is a duck", Mel finished behind him, wrapping her arms around his waist, "so what looks like a duck"?

Turning around to face her, he cupped her chin, "just a saying Joel favours", he winked, placing a quick kiss on her lips. "Does your sister take sugar"?

"Just one".

"One it is", he turned back, spooning the sugar in, "here you go", he handed her the mugs, grabbing his and heading towards the backdoor.

"Not joining us"?

"No, I'll leave you to your girlie chat, I have a couple of calls to make", raising his hand with his phone in it, "I'll be out there if you need me".

Walking back to the front room with the tea she sat down again, handing one to Sarah.

"He seems really nice, you've got a good one there".

"I know", Mel smiled sadly at her.

"Don't do that", Sarah wiggled her finger admonishingly, "it's okay to be happy, and I won't let you taint this with guilt". Taking a sip of her tea, she continued. "And as you so rightly pointed out, this is no-one's fault but Rich's". "Anyway, enough about that, how's the progress on Lucy's party dress going"?

"It's finished and even if I do say so myself, it looks fantastic", she beamed, "where is Lucy, by the way"?

"Dropped her off for a play date at her friend's on my way over".

"Little minx couldn't wait for me to leave her, I'm sure she thought I was cramping her style".

"Want to see it"? Jumping up, she headed into her craft room, returning moments later with the dress. "Here it is", she swept it out in front of her dramatically.

"Oh sis, it's beautiful, she'll love it", reaching out to touch the fabric as if it were fragile, "you always had a talent for sewing, I on the other hand, couldn't sew to save my life". "I remember grandmother trying her best to teach me, but I always wanted to run and play, a self-confessed tomboy", she grinned at the memory.

"If I recall correctly, you shined at her cookery lessons though", Melody chuckled, memories of them standing on the kitchen chairs stirring bowls of gloop around, more flour on their faces and hands than in the bowls, while their grandmother patiently instructed them.

"Well, if you're going to make something, might as well be something you can eat", she teased. "I could see the sense in that, unfortunately I always had a healthy appetite", she moaned, tapping her stomach and winking at Mel. "Now, if I had those extra three inches of height", she laughed as Mel rolled her eyes at the familiar tease.

"You'd be just the same", she played back.

"Except taller", Sarah finished for her.

They spent the next hour reminiscing about old times, while pouring over old photo albums that had belonged to their grandmother, the mood happy and light as they laughed at the photos of their young selves.

Glancing at her watch, Sarah made to get up. "Got to go", she sighed, placing the photo album on the coffee table. "I'm meeting a friend in town", she clarified, glancing at Mel's questioning look, "a bit of retail therapy's good for the soul".

"But hell for the bank balance", Mel laughingly retorted, linking arms with her and walking to the front door.

"Take care love, say goodbye to Alex for me", Sarah spoke softly, hugging her tight.

"I will, you too sis, and have fun shopping", she squeezed her back. It was so good to have her feisty sister back, she mused as she stood there waving her off, the heavy feeling of guilt that had plagued her evaporating as she headed back inside.

Checking on the marinating salmon fillets in the fridge, she replaced the foil wrapping, pleased with herself. She would be serving them on a bed of baby potatoes, leeks and a creamy sauce, following her grandmother's well-worn recipe to the letter, she felt quietly confident in its success. "Hopefully, it will turn out well, gran", she mused aloud, moving the bowl of fresh mixed rocket salad to a higher shelf. It would be a great side dish, a balsamic dressing and a little shaved parmesan would make it perfect, the fact that it had come straight from Alex's garden, an added bonus. She smiled at the memory, his pleasure had been evident as he had handed them to her 'grew these myself, thought they'd go well with dinner', his boyish smile of pride melting her heart.

Grabbing two bottles of beer and uncapping them, she headed into the garden to find Alex stretched out on a lounger, his sunglasses perched up on his head as he flipped through a file.

"Sarah gone already"? He smiled, shutting his file and accepting the beer she held out to him.

"Yes, she just left, she said to say goodbye to you".

"Well, if the laughter I heard was anything to go by, I'd say you both had a good time".

"We did, I'm glad she called round", she settled onto the lounger taking a large gulp of beer.

"It's good to see you smiling again", he gazed at her, the warmth in his voice reflecting in his eyes.

The day had passed pleasantly, they had eaten their lunch in the garden and that afternoon Alex had driven them to the hardware store, where Melody had selected paints and dust sheets for the planned re-decorating of the front room, which Alex had insisted on painting with her the following day. A walk in the park had followed with Toby being his usual energetic self, insisting on Alex to throw the ball till they all headed wearily home.

As Melody busily prepared the dinner, she felt a contented glow wash over her; the domestic bliss seemed to envelop her as she all but danced around the kitchen to Mantovani's 'The Melba Waltz' that Alex had selected to play, the cascading strings of the music sending her mind into romantic overdrive as she imagined dancing with him in her rose-pink gown.

The first guest to arrive was Lindsey; she swept into the kitchen, two bottles of wine in her hands, "I come armed", holding out the wine, the laugh dying as she glimpsed Melody's barely disguised bruised face. "Oh hun, what happened"?

"It's a long story", she sighed, filling her in as she shaved parmesan over the rocket salad.

"I'll kill him", Lindsey fumed, her usual soft demeanour turning ferocious.

"No you won't, it's all being sorted".

"Who are we killing", Charlotte's playful voice chimed in as she entered the kitchen, dressed in crop jeans and a purple and blue tie dye t-shirt, her short spiky hair tipped with matching shades of blue.

"No-one's killing anyone", Melody admonished, turning to Charlotte.

"Wow, that's a shiner", she whistled, looking at Melody's bruises, a warning look from Lindsey momentarily silencing her. "At least we're all colour co-ordinated", she teased, pulling at her t-shirt and glancing at Lindsey's blue jersey dress, and then at Mel.

"But she's wearing pink", Lindsey admonished, frowning at the mischievous twinkle in Lottie's eyes.

"She means my bruises", Mel giggled, the fraught atmosphere evaporating as they all laughed at Charlotte's incorrigible wit.

Joel followed soon after and the drinks soon flowed, the happy chatter and laughter making Melody finally relax; this had been just what she needed, she thought, smiling as she watched Alex holding the floor, regaling them all with tales of his and Joel's air-force days. His handsome face alight with the stories he told, every now and then their glances meeting and a secret small smile would light his eyes, drawing her in and holding her breathlessly rapt.

"So, Joel, what's with the wings tatt"? Charlotte asked, leaning into him and pulling at his t-shirt sleeve, a mischievous twinkle in her eyes.

"Put him down Lottie", Lindsey playfully berated, rolling her eyes.

"Aw, come on Lind's, don't you want to know too", she batted her eyes at her, turning back to Joel, she glanced at him coyly, "you don't mind do you"?

"Not at all", he grinned at her and then at Lindsey, "it's from my air-force days when I served in the RAF, these are swift wings", he pointed to his arm at the two years tattooed in the middle of the wings, "this is the year I joined and this one when I left, a reminder of my time served".

"So you served for twelve years", she calculated, peering closely at the tattoo, "and do you have the real thing"?

"I do", he nodded solemnly, "we all get them once we have completed our training".

"Do you have one too", she turned to look directly at Alex.

"Wings yes, tattoo no".

Turning back to Joel, she smiled sweetly. "So Joel, you got any pets"? The combined roar of laughter from Lindsey and Melody caused him to frown questionably at Alex, who simply shrugged his shoulders and raised his hands in defeat. A startled Toby waking up and shoving his toy at Joel, sent them into fresh laughter.

Leaving them to their conversation, Melody headed back to the kitchen, the laughter still shaking her frame. Pulling out plates from the dresser, she placed them on the kitchen side.

"Looks like they're all behaving themselves", Alex's seductive voice warmed her neck as he came up behind her, "how are you holding up"? He growled low as he nibbled at her earlobe.

"Mm fine", she relaxed back against him, his warm hands seeming to burn through the thin material of her shift dress, quickening her pulse. "I'm glad you told Joel about my incident before he came, I don't think I could have gone through all that again".

"I thought as much", he paused turning her to face him, "so, what's with the joke".

"Joke"? She frowned momentarily confused.

"Yes, when she asked if Joel had any pets", he whispered, a smile tugging at his mouth.

"Oh that", she grinned, her eyes sparkling mischievously, "it's Lottie's theory on men", lowering her voice, she continued, "if a guy has a pet, he's more likely to be stable, therefore good boyfriend material".

"We better get him a cat then", Alex murmured, his laugh rumbling through her.

The rest of the evening passed smoothly, with dinner a resounding success. After seeing the last of the guests off, Alex made his way back to the kitchen, leaning on the door jamb, he watched as Melody loaded the last of the dishes into the dishwasher, all the while keeping an overly interested Toby at bay as he tried in vain to lick at the plates. Closing the door and switching it on, she turned to catch him staring at her, a smile playing around his lips.

"That went well", he mused, pushing away from the door and heading over to her.

"It sure did, and I think we have a budding new romance", she sighed, reaching up to trace her fingers over his stubbled jaw, the feel of it like fine sandpaper against her fingertips.

"I guess she's willing to by-pass the pet theory this time", he groaned, playfully capturing her fingers in his mouth.

"I think you guess right", she murmured back, wrapping her free arm around his neck, a look of desire flooding her eyes.

Chapter 13

Alex awoke with a start, the nightmare still fresh in his mind, images of Melody slipping away from him as he tried to grasp onto her hands, the cold faceless stranger pulling her deeper and deeper into the crowds, his knife glinting menacingly at her throat as her wide frightened eyes beseeched him for help, but he couldn't move as he tried, his legs seemed to catch on something. He sat up, untangling the sheet that had twisted around them. "Pull it together", he groaned, wiping the sleep from his eyes as he glanced around his room, the familiar space quiet and empty. Annoyed at himself for letting the nightmare get to him, he tossed the covers back and swung out of bed, the troubling thoughts of the thief and now this Richard incident had really got to him, all he wanted to do was check on Mel and drown out the images of his nightmare. Pulling on his running shorts and selecting a new t-shirt, he hurriedly dressed, grabbing his phone and shoving it in his pocket. He rushed downstairs, locating his runners at the back door, he looked around his chrome and black kitchen, so different from Mel's, no pot plants on the windowsill or children's paintings on the fridge held in place with goofy magnets; not for the first time, Alex decided he didn't like the clinical look of his kitchen. Shoving his bare feet into his runners and picking up Mel's keys, he locked his back door and headed over the fence to her cottage, the pull on him to check on her too strong to deny.

The cottage was quiet as he let himself in; walking into the kitchen, Toby's low growl greeted him. "It's just me, boy", Alex whispered, closing the door silently behind him. Did he just imagine it or did Toby sag with relief as he settled back down on hearing Alex's voice; shaking his head hopelessly at his overactive imagination, he walked to the hallway. Taking the stairs two at a time, he hesitated outside of her bedroom door, quietly opening it, he peered inside. She lay curled in a foetal position in the centre of the double bed, her golden hair splayed over the pillows; silently he crept over to the bed, a slight smile played at her lips as she dreamed, her thick lashes twitching slightly as he tentatively brushed a kiss over her flushed cheeks. The relief he felt at the sight of her sleeping peacefully, soon warred with the feeling of guilt for having intruded into her space; quietly retracing his steps, he exited her room, making his way to the kitchen, he opened the back door for Toby.

Breathing in the crisp morning air, he stood watching the dog wander around the garden, his nightmare receding with every breath. The first night of staying back at home and he was acting like a fool, he berated himself; heading back in, he filled the coffee pot and grabbed his phone from his pocket, a couple of text message alerts appearing on his screen, one from Joel and one from an unknown number. Opening Joel's, he smiled as he read, 'hi mate, great fun last night. Could you forward me pixie's number, thanks'.

Sending a reply with Charlotte's number, he then opened the unknown number's text, 'hello Alex, I'm afraid I don't have any old birthday cards or documents. About meeting Jack, I'd really like to do that soon' Christina.

Adding her number to his contacts, he texted her back, promising to arrange a meeting for the following week. Grabbing a notepad and pen from the dresser, he scribbled down a quick reminder to arrange it. Dropping the pen, he headed over to the coffee pot and poured out two mugs, a low whine from Toby brought his attention to the dog, who had reappeared at the back door and was now pawing at his empty bowl. "Okay boy, I get it", he huffed, grabbing the kibble from the cupboard and pouring a generous bowl full for him, patting his back fondly as his nose disappeared into his bowl, his tail swishing as he crunched merrily away. Fixing Mel some toast and a bowl of cereal, he arranged it on a tray, stepping out into the garden, he took a quick look around and he found what he wanted, snapping a simple pink flower, he headed back inside and found a small flute vase under the sink. Placing the flower in it, he added it to the tray, a glass of fresh orange juice and he was set.

"Morning beautiful", he beamed, settling the tray down beside the bed, the mattress dipping as he sat on the side, making her roll slightly towards him.

"Alex", she murmured, looking at him beneath her lashes, a slow smile spreading on her face, "thought I was dreaming you up", she yawned, reaching out to him, a blush blooming on her already flushed face.

"Good dreams, I hope", he smiled, brushing her golden curls off her face and trailing his fingers down her neck.

"Mm, good dreams", she sighed, sitting up to look at him, "you brought me breakfast"? Her voice sounding husky as she cast a look at the tray.

"Yes, and a flower for my girl too", he laughed, picking up the tray and placing it on her lap, "I thought I'd take Toby with me for a run", he paused, downing his coffee, "you relax and enjoy your breakfast, we'll be back soon", he stood stretching out his leg muscles.

"Oh my, breakfast and a show", she laughed.

"Anything for milady's smile", he teased, wiggling his hips at her, quickly side-stepping the pillow as she threw it at him. "Now that's no way to treat your gallant knight", he chuckled, heading out of the bedroom as she made to throw another one at him, her laughter following him as he descended the stairs.

The boot fair was buzzing, even the threat of rain hadn't put people off from coming. Melody looked skyward, the blue sky and small white clouds belying any threat of rain, she smiled to herself, glad the weatherman had got it wrong once again. Heading towards a stall, the bright colours catching her eyes, she picked out some red, white and blue tulle. She guessed she could probably make up at least fifty scrunchies with the material, the no sew style she had in mind would be quick to make and with her unexpected time off, she would have plenty of time; the fact that they would sell like hot cakes in the shop with the queen's diamond jubilee just around the corner another bonus. Mentally dressing the shop in the red, white and blue bunting, she calculated the time it would take to overhaul the shop into a jubilee theme, the union jack paper she had just purchased would look great banded around the leftover homemade candles Susie had made for the shop last year. Feeling pleased with herself and her plans, she headed towards the burger vendor's stand; ordering two colas she found a seat and sat down, closing her eyes and lifting her face to the warmth of the sun.

Toby was pushing his nose into her legs, a huge green crocodile stuffed toy firmly wedged in his mouth, brought her out of her daydreams. "What you got there", she laughed as the over-sized toy dropped at her feet.

"I couldn't stop him", Alex laughed, walking up to them, a resigned look on his face as he dropped into the seat next to her.

"That's the biggest prize yet", she laughed, eyeing the crocodile as Toby partially lay over it, chewing at its leg. "What's that"? Melody asked, looking enquiringly at a large metal bar wrapped in paper at Alex's feet.

"Got a replacement blade for my lawnmower", he grinned, "the stall over there sells parts and tools, I nearly came away with a whole new tool box collection".

"And yet, you only have a blade, very restrained of you", she teased, handing him a can of cola.

"I know, might go back over for more", he cast a wayward glance back at the stall.

"It's got you", she laughed as he raised a questioning eyebrow, "the lure of the boot fair, no-one leaves empty handed, or with just one item".

"You're right minx, I'm hooked", he laughingly confessed, throwing his arms up in surrender. Melody closed her eyes, the sun's rays warming her face as she tilted her face skywards, the day was turning out to be a pleasant one. Alex had dropped Toby home after his run, heading back home to shower and change and then surprising her with his eagerness to come to the boot fair with her, a fact that still made her smile. She had lost count of the Sunday mornings she had made this solitary journey with just Toby for company, never once thinking it might hold any interest for Alex. But here they were and he seemed to be enjoying himself.

"What are you after boy", Alex frowned, looking at Toby as he pushed his nose into melody's bag.

"Oh I'm sorry boy, I forgot", she exclaimed peeking at the two of them, reaching for her bag and taking out his water bowl, "he needs a drink too", she explained to Alex, pouring out some water for him. "There you go", she soothed, placing it on the ground for him.

"Not making a very good job at this pet daddy lark am I"? Alex grimaced jokingly.

"I'd say you're doing a fine job, after all that's the biggest toy he's ever managed to wangle out of a boot fair before", her infectious laughter rubbing off on him as Toby drank thirstily whilst keeping an eye on them both.

They spent the next hour wandering between the stalls; Alex had given in and bought a few tools he claimed he needed, although she was sure she had seen remarkably similar ones in his toolbox at home.

"A man can never have too many tools", he had laughed at her teasing when he had stopped once again to look at a collection of claw hammers laid out in size order. Picking different ones up and replacing them as he thoughtfully rotated them, choosing a black and yellow handled one, he paid the stall owner and grinned sheepishly at Melody. "I didn't have a curved headed one", his grin lighting up his face.

"Well, it's good you got one now", she laughed, linking her hand with his as they continued strolling along the stalls, only half paying attention to the different contents each one offered.

"You want to get out of here", Alex suggested thirty minutes later as they exited another row.

"I think so, I've got all I need", she gestured to her carrier bags full of purchases.

Scooping her bags from her, he placed them on his wrist and flung his free arm around her shoulder. "Allow me, milady", his tone of voice was theatrical as he led her to the car.

Timothy paced back and forth in his small bedsit; less than a week to go till the gala and he still hadn't had any luck securing a position as a waiter. The visit to the A1 agency had left him nervous, the way the receptionist had treated him made his senses prickle. She had seemed wary of him as she clutched his file to her, the green post-it note on the front was new; it was almost like she hadn't wanted him to see it but he had, the post-it note had just one word that spooked him, 'query'. He was glad he had ducked out of there sharpish, before he had enquired about the gala job, relief now settling on him that he had registered at the agency under his mother's maiden name, no bread crumb trail would ever lead to him leaving him in the clear when his plans unfolded. Fortunately, while she had been off checking who could see him that day, he had spied the folder sitting blatantly on her desk, the gala logo emblazoned on the front, a quick look and he had memorised a few of the familiar names scheduled to work as waiting staff for the event. "Well, there's more than one way to skin a cat", he muttered, stopping mid-stride as an idea started to form, an evil smile splitting his face.

Arriving at the little pub, he grabbed a beer and settled into a corner, watching, and waiting. He knew this watering hole was favoured by the men who worked at the temping agency; seeing his target finally walk in, he observed his short blonde spikey hair and casual clothes, he was about the same height as himself and had a slim build. "Yes, this could definitely work", he quietly mused to himself as he casually made his way to the bar.

"Owen", he smiled, tapping his arm as the younger man swung around to the greeting.

"Um, do I know you"?

"It's Tim, we worked together out at the golf club".

"Oh yes, I remember, didn't you work at the bar with me", he frowned, obviously trying to place him. Timothy nodded at the fictitious story, glad that Owen had not caught him in the lie.

"Never did get to say thanks", Timothy smiled at his outrageous lie.

"Thanks for what"?

"You covered for me when I messed up that order, would have been fired on the spot if it hadn't been for you". Knowing full well that he had read Owen right as he readily accepted the praise. He had worked with him on one occasion and the jumped-up little yes-man had taken all the credit for everyone else's hard work that day doing his utmost to impress the management, sucking up to them in a nauseating way.

"You're welcome", he smiled, turning back to his beer.

"Let me get you a drink", Timothy enthused, raising his hand to attract the barman. Ordering them both another round, he raised his glass to him. "Here's to you, a real gent in this cut-throat agency work". Taking a gulp of his beer, Timothy eyed his target. He looked like he was lapping it all up, like taking candy from a baby, he thought cynically leaning in for his killer line. "So you got any good jobs coming up"?

Walking back to his bedsit, Timothy praised himself on his plan, several beers into his discussion with Owen, he had gleaned all he had needed. Suffering the pompous fool's bragging was well worth it, he acknowledged to himself, he now had his address and work schedule, everything he would need to make his plan work. "Silly fool, you deserve what's coming your way", he laughed as he entered his drab bedsit.

Sitting on the floor of her craft room, the tulle fabric surrounding her, Melody cut strips of each of the three colours, tying them onto the elastic band in the red, white and blue pattern, then repeating the sequence, until she had a full scrunchie. Pleased with her efforts, she started another, it was a while later as she sat back admiring her pile of growing scrunchies. She heard Alex starting up the lawn mower, he had been off to his cottage, eager to fix his new blade to it as soon as they had arrived home earlier; now as she heard the engine roaring, she decided he must be done fixing it. A tall glass of juice and a slice of cake suddenly seemed very appealing, and knowing Alex, he would be thirsty too. Uncurling her legs, she stepped carefully over her material and made her way to the kitchen, the back door stood wide open, a gentle breeze ruffling Toby's fur as he lay in the doorway, his crocodile wedged against the door jamb and under his head. Reaching into the fridge, Melody pulled out a carton of fresh pineapple juice and a bottle of lemonade. Retrieving two tall glasses from the dresser, she mixed the two drinks; adding ice cubes, she placed them on the tray. Cutting two slices of the coffee cake she had made earlier that day, she placed them onto the plates and added them to the tray, she carefully stepped over Toby carrying it to the garden and setting it down on the garden table.

Alex, seeing Melody waving at him, cut the mower's engine and hopped over the fence and strolled over; dressed only in low slung jean shorts and runners, she noticed how his bare torso glistened in the sun, his six-pack barely concealed by the light scattering of hair, the muscles contracting in his strong powerful legs as he made his way to her held her attention. Grabbing his discarded t-shirt from the back of the lounger, he wiped the sweat from his face, throwing it back down as he settled beside her, taking the offered drink and downing half of it. She watched mesmerised, as his Adam's apple moved rhythmically up and down.

"I needed that", he drawled, a lazy smile splitting his lips.

"You sure did", she shyly smiled back, a feeling of being caught staring making her blush.

"And cake too, I'm going to have to watch myself", he teased, tapping his flat stomach, loving the way he could make her blush so easily. She was adorable, he mused, taking a moment to drink her in as she sat next to him, her head lowered, her hair falling forward covering her face. Dressed in a simple white shirt dress, a belt cinched at her small waist with little yellow embroidered daisies winding down the sides disappearing at the slits, revealing her long golden legs, he struggled to dampen his wayward thinking, reaching instead for his slice of cake. "How's the scrunchie making going", he asked, wiping crumbs from his lips.

"I've made quite a few, still loads more to make though", she smiled, taking a delicate bite of cake and licking her fork thoughtfully, "the new blade seems to have been a success".

"Yes, it was quite straightforward to attach, I was going to cut your grass next, if you want", he inclined his head at her lawn. The grass overgrown with a profusion of daisies popping up everywhere, it sure needed a cut, her old electric lawnmower having given up the last time she had used it.

"That would be great, I still haven't replaced my old mower" Another job to add to her to do list, she made a mental note.

"Should only take me thirty minutes, then we can start in the front room".

"We're still going to paint it then"? She frowned, thinking of the task ahead.

"Yes, I moved all the furniture to the centre of the room and covered it in dust sheets already", he paused taking the last bite of cake, "won't take us long, I have all the paint trays and rollers to get ready, then we can start. I just need you to take down your photos and trinkets off of the mantel piece".

"Okay, I'll do that, and finish a few more scrunchies", she sighed, standing and collecting their plates.

"Maybe change into paint gear too, wouldn't want you to ruin that nice dress", he mused, caressing her with his eyes.

"Yes boss", she playfully flung over her shoulder at him as she made her way indoors, his low throaty chuckle following her, sending goosebumps of excitement over her body. "That man", she proclaimed to Toby, rolling her eyes as he followed her looking hopefully at the empty plates, a smile breaking her frown. "Ah, come here boy", she scooted down and hugged the dog tight, "what are we going to do with him"? She mused, ruffling his ears. Hearing the lawn mower's engine starting up, she quickly stood. "Best get those photos down now boy", she grabbed an empty box from her craft room and headed to the front room.

Chapter 14

The days flew by; they had finished painting the front room on Monday, and she had got lots of scrunchies made up. Alex had spent the weekend by her side, planning the next room to decorate and noting little jobs he would do around the cottage for her. By mid-week, Melody found herself rushed off her feet at the shop, the scrunchies had been a huge success and had nearly sold out. She was glad she had thought to keep one tucked in her bag for Lucy, thinking of her niece, she stole a quick look at her mobile phone. She hadn't heard from Sarah since Saturday, a worried frown settled on her face, maybe she could call in to see her after work; an uneasy feeling settling over her, three days and no contact. Well, maybe she was just busy with her new life, she mused, deciding she was just over-reacting.

But try as she might all day, she could not seem to shake the feeling, finally giving in to the feelings, she gathered her bag and keys.

"Suse, I'm going to head off early, you okay to lock up"?

"Sure thing, Mel, see you tomorrow", Susie's sing-song voice reassured her. Heading out with Toby, Melody opened her car, securing Toby in the back. "I'm sure she's fine, ay boy", she muttered, trying to calm her frayed nerves.

The drive over to Sarah's house went fast, different scenarios playing out in her head, each making her more and more worried. Pulling into her drive, she bounded up to the front door, repeatedly pressing the bell.

"Okay, I'm coming", a terse Sarah called out as she headed towards the door. Opening it, she glowered out, her face softening on seeing Melody standing there. "What's up, Mel"? She questioned, looking at her worried face, stepping back to let her in.

"Oh sis, I've been so worried about you, are you okay? You haven't called for three days", Melody gushed, hugging her sister tight, feeling silly at her overactive imagination.

"I'm fine love, I've just been so busy with all that's been going on", she paused, stepping back to look at her, "come into the kitchen, I'll fix us a coffee and you can tell me what's got you in such a state".

Sitting at the kitchen island, Melody watched as her sister fixed them both a drink. She looked well and confident, she thought finally calming down.

"So what was that all about", Sarah soothed, pushing a mug of coffee into her hands.

"I'm just jumpy, I guess, and when I hadn't heard from you for the past few days, I got it into my head that something terrible might have happened".

"I guess it's to be expected with all that you've been through, but I'm fine", she reassured her, "I'm sorry I haven't called, I've just been trying to give you some space", she grimaced, "I can see now, I should have got in touch sooner".

Melody sat looking at her sister; she was dressed in smart black trousers and a turquoise blouse, her new cropped hair and new style of clothes still so alien to her.

"You look so different", she blurted out, embarrassed at having been caught staring so openly.

"I do, don't I", Sarah smiled, smoothing her hands over her hips, "I found out today that I got the job". A look of triumph was shining from her eyes.

"Oh that's wonderful sis, when do you start"?

"They want me to start on Tuesday, I've been so busy getting everything organised", she paused, sipping her coffee, "Lucy's excited too, she thinks it will mean more play dates with her new best friend. She's been spending more time over at their house, whilst I get everything sorted".

Leaning in, Melody reached over and held her sister's hand. "How is she coping with all this Richard business"?

Sarah stiffened slightly. "She's asked a couple of times where her daddy is but seems content enough with my explanation that he's gone to live in another home", the far off look in her eyes ending the conversation. Low growls from Toby and Rex shattered the awkward silence as they both bit hold of a rather worn toy and started to play tug with it.

Reaching for her bag, Melody pulled out the scrunchie. "I made this for Lucy", she smiled brightly, presenting the red, white and blue scrunchie, "it's for the diamond jubilee, they've nearly sold out in the shop".

Taking the scrunchie, Sarah examined it, pulling at the elastic band. "Oh she will be thrilled with this, they are doing a project at school on the jubilee, it's all she talks about lately".

"Alex says it's going to be busy for his firm because of this four-day weekend diamond jubilee, what with the gala happening at the same time as well". Sarah looked over her mug at her sister, pleased that the bruises on her face now faded and had almost gone, the sun from the patio doors turning her hair into a halo of gold, a short coral pink shift dress with puff sleeves and criss cross frills beneath the bust line showed her figure off to its best advantage, her matching painted coral pink toenails peeking out from her cream espadrille sandals. Matching fingernails wrapped around her coffee mug completed the look.

"You've lost weight", Sarah mused, still looking at her, a concerned look settling on her face.

"I know, I've had to take the gown in an inch", Mel grimaced, absentmindedly tugging at her dress.

"Well you're looking good, but try not to lose anymore, or there'll be nothing left of you", she admonished, tilting her head to the side and flicking her bangs out of her eyes.

They chatted for a while, the light-hearted banter making them both at ease.

"I better get going". Mel stood grabbing her bag and calling to Toby.

"Oh, I almost forgot", Sarah moaned racing over to her sideboard, "Lucy drew another picture for you", handing it over to her, Mel gazed down at two figures and a dog. "It's Alex, you and Toby", she grinned at the look of pleasure on Mel's face.

"Oh how sweet, tell her, I'll add it to my fridge door".

Glancing at her watch, Sarah tutted. "I've got to get going too, she'll be finished at school soon".

Walking out of the house together, they promised to stay in touch, hugging tightly until they both parted, hurrying to their cars. Waving madly at each other, Mel drove away, the light-hearted feeling continuing as she drove home.

Joel pulled his car into the only available parking space in the busy residential street, the houses looked worn and old. Green and black overflowing wheelie bins dotted the pavement; checking the piece of paper, he noted the number he was looking for. By his quick calculations, number eighty-six, Albert Street should be three doors down. Grabbing his clipboard and locking his car, he headed slowly towards the house; no white vans, he mused, scanning both sides of the street. Arriving at number eighty-six, he took in the scruffy small stone front garden, the blue paint chipping on the front door, tired net curtains hanging limply at the dirty bay windows. A tabby cat sat on the low wall, watching warily as he walked up to the front door.

Gripping his clipboard tighter, he rang the bell and waited. The door opened, revealing a young woman standing there, a scowl on her face; peering in, he noted a communal hallway showing different numbered internal doors. Bedsits, he quickly surmised. "Can I help you", she enquired, squinting in the sunlight and looking suspiciously at his clipboard.

"Hi there, I'm looking for a…", he glanced at his clipboard, "a Mr Tim Abbott".

She stepped forward, frowning at him. "And you are"? She snapped, seeming not at all pleased to be being disturbed.

Turning on a killer watt smile, he went into his role. "I'm from the A1 Employment Agency, Tim's on our books for an up-coming event. I just need to go through a couple of items with him".

"He's not here, don't know when he'll be back either", she pre-empted him, starting to close the door.

"Well, if he does turn up, will you give him this", he handed her his fake business card, the burner phone number emblazoned on the front.

"Okay", she reluctantly took the card and shut the front door.

Heading back to his car, he punched out a number. "It's Joel, yes it's the address, but he's not here, from what I could make out it's bedsits", he spoke softly to the recipient on the phone. "Let Alex know and have him send someone to watch it, as soon as he can". Ending the call, he jumped into his car and pulled away.

Melody headed into the department store, having taken Toby home, she had decided that a bit of retail therapy was just what she needed. Having purchased some underwear to wear under the gown, she felt pleased with her purchases. Wandering around, browsing, she selected some new chocolate bronze eye shadow and a golden quartz pencil eyeliner that the salesgirl assured her would bring out the amber in her hazel eyes. Heading to the perfume counter, she tried several samples, deciding on a bottle of Beautiful and matching body lotion by Estee Lauder, the delicate floral and vanilla notes reminding her of summertime and romance. Heading over to the hair salon, she booked an appointment for Saturday afternoon, deciding on an up-do, the stylist explained how they could pin her hair up and let a few curls escape to frame her face, the diamante clips Melody had bought that day would be scattered throughout creating a stunning effect.

Leaving the hair salon, Melody felt her excitement building up, her shopping and the hair appointment had gone better than she had expected. With only two days until the gala, everything was slotting nicely into place; stopping to gaze in at the jeweller's, she felt her excitement turn to nervousness at the thought of wearing the emerald necklace. Shrugging off the fluttering nerves, she made her way back to the car, the excitement of the gala and her purchases drowning out her doubts, the image of herself in the rose pink gown, her hair swept up and her black venetian shawl draped over her shoulders, played over in her mind. "I really will feel like a princess", she mused, flicking the radio on. Glancing at her face in the mirror, she fingered the now barely visible bruises; so glad that they would be gone in time for the gala. Kelly Clarkson's 'Stronger' started to play on the radio and she cranked the volume up as she drove away, singing along to the chorus, yes 'what doesn't kill you makes you stronger, stand a little taller', she thought as she belted out the lyrics, feeling defiant and confident.

Alex paced back and forth in his office, the news from Joel had been good; now he had arranged for Peter, one of their workers, to watch Tim Abbotts' home. It would only be a matter of time till they had him under surveillance, if he so much as sneezed in the wrong direction, they would know. He checked the security detail of the up-coming gala for what felt like the millionth time, everything looked good. He just could not seem to shake his feeling of unease, he impatiently pressed the intercom. "Jane, I'm heading out to check the security layout of the Crafton Hotel again. When Joel comes back, will you let him know I'll be heading home after".

"Sure boss, no problem", Jane's voice crackled over the intercom. Grabbing his keys and phone, he headed out to his car.

After doing a walkthrough of the hotel and double checking every detail with the manager hovering patiently by his side ready to answer any and all of his questions, Alex finally relaxed, "all looks good here". Alex informed the manager, who nodded and smiled, a look of relief on his face. With just a couple of last-minute adjustments sorted out with the manager, he left the hotel, his mobile beeping pulled him from his reflections and scowling at it, he read the text from Jane.

"Hey boss, don't forget to pick up your tux from the dry cleaner's", a smiley face emoji finishing the text making him smile. A glance at his watch made him hurry his step, he would just about make it. Texting a quick thank you back to Jane, he gunned his SUV and headed towards the dry cleaners.

Melody stood looking at herself in her full length mirror, the gown she wore transforming her into someone she could barely recognise. The rose-pink satin bodice peeked out beneath the black venetian lace that fitted over it, hugging her body, the sweetheart neckline hinting at her full cleavage. Touching her neck, she imagined the emerald necklace placed there; it would look so startling against her lightly sun-tanned skin. Worrying her bottom lip, she turned and scooped up the black Venetian lace wrap, draping it over her arms. "We'll damn well get him, Christina", she swore, standing a bit taller and lifting her chin defiantly, the words of the song she had sung on the way home strengthening her resolve.

Taking the gown off, she hung it back on her wardrobe door. Pulling on a pair of jogger pants and a fresh t-shirt, she sat at her dressing table, emptying the new make-up from the bag. She looked at her scrubbed face, the bruises now barely visible. Tying her hair up into a messy bun, she leaned into the mirror and applied her new makeup. The sales girl had been right, she thought staring at her eyes, the gold picked out the amber in them; her sultry eyes looking so different from what she was used to seeing.

The new lipstick worked perfectly with the look, just adding a touch of colour to her full lips; smiling at herself, she thought of Sarah, 'the rule of makeup', her sister would always state 'if you have dramatic eyes your lipstick should always be subtle, or run the risk of looking like a clown' taking a quick selfie, she added a quick text, "trying out gala make-up", and sent the photo to Sarah. The ping from her mobile was almost instant as she looked at Sarah's reply.

"Beautiful sis, don't forget a little blusher". Picking up another brush, she applied a little blusher to her cheekbones, then rubbed most of it off leaving just a trace of it behind. "No clowns here, sis", she laughed, standing to leave.

Heading downstairs, she met Toby waiting for her at the bottom. "Hey boy, what do you think", she crooned, hunkering down beside him and dramatically batting her eyes, his wagging tail thumping against her leg as he snuffled his nose into her his only response. "Glad you approve", she laughed, leading him to the kitchen and grabbing his bowl. Scooping some dog food into it, she placed it down for him. The sound of Toby crunching his food followed her around the kitchen as she poured a glass of wine and pinned up Lucy's drawing on the fridge, the picture bringing thoughts of Alex to her mind as she headed into her craft room.

Timothy turned the van into his street, the bottle of whiskey he had purchased safely stowed on the passenger seat, tapping his jacket pocket he felt the packet of sleeping pills still there. His plan was so easy, he smiled, pleased with himself, a few glasses of spiked whiskey and then Owen would be rendered unconscious for at least eight hours, and the beauty of it, he would have no memories of it, just a bad hangover, leaving Timothy in the clear. A sense of foreboding crept over him as he neared his bedsit, the navy sedan car parked across from his house seemed out of place, the man sitting in it slunk low in the seat, stepping on the accelerator, he sped past only easing up when he was sure he was not being followed.

He knew every neighbour's car in his street, and he had a sixth sense that this was not a coincidence, he was sure now he was being watched. "Not today, arseholes", he grimaced, angrily pulling into the underground car park and killing the engine. Pacing around the shops, he killed time watching for anything out of place. After buying a few necessities and stowing them in the van, he decided he would have to check out if the sedan was still parked by his house. Two hours later, he made his way back to his street on foot, turning into his street, he skulked partway down the path coming from behind where the sedan had been parked. "Damn", he swore as he spied the sedan still parked in the same place, the man still sat hunkered down in the seat, his head trained on Timothy's house. Turning abruptly, he headed back to the underground car park. "Now what", he mused, knowing that returning to his bedsit was out of the question. Two days until he could execute his plan, so close to his goal, he could not be rumbled now. Grabbing his phone, he looked at hostels close to him, selecting the cheapest one. He started his van and headed to it. Laying low was going to cost him but he would not risk blowing his plans now.

Chapter 15

Melody sat in her garden, the morning sun warming her, dressed in aqua shorts and a white spaghetti strapped t-shirt, she decided a little break was just what she needed. The morning so far had been busy, she had laid out her gown and underwear for the gala that evening. Alex would pick her up at seven, bringing with him the emerald necklace for her to wear, and escort her to the gala at the hotel. She double checked that her hair appointment was booked for later that afternoon, with last minute nerves causing butterflies to stomp around in her stomach, she kept herself busy with housework that had taken up a nice bit of her time. Now swinging her legs onto the lounger, she relaxed back, watching as Toby rolled on his back, rubbing a smell he seemed to find intriguing all over himself.

Her thoughts turned to Alex, making her smile as the memories of yesterday's visit to Christina washed over her; they had spent Friday afternoon reuniting Christina and Jack. Picking up a nervous Jack and driving him to Christina's had felt overwhelmingly surreal as Alex made small talk, trying to ease Jack's nervousness. Later, watching as they had embraced, it was as if all the years apart had simply melted away. She felt a lump in her throat as the touching scene replayed in her mind, the look of love in their eyes undeniable. Alex had squeezed her hand as if knowing she was imagining them at that age. Excusing themselves, they had gone for a walk in Christina's garden, she could almost smell the sweet scent of roses as if she were still there now. Taking a seat on the stone bench, they had enjoyed the quiet garden, holding hands, no words had been necessary; it felt like love was in the air. He had turned to face her and the look in his eyes had almost stopped her heart, remembering the look, she felt her toes curl in delight, the way he raised her hand to his lips and kissed each finger, never once breaking eye contact.

"I love you Melody", his voice was rough with emotion. The moment magical, sitting in the beautiful garden surrounded by flowers, a rose archway as a backdrop, would stay with her always.

"I love you too", she had whispered back. The kiss had been so tender and full of love, she felt herself falling even deeper in love.

Jack and Christina had found them sitting there gazing at one another, a chuckle from Jack alerting them to their presence.

"Love is definitely in the air", Jack quoted, his arm around Christina as they smiled down at them. They had made a stunning looking couple, she had thought looking at them. His tall athletic frame dwarfing Christina's small frame, his distinguished grey hair and moustache belying his age, light blue eyes twinkling mischievously at them. Holding Christina close to him, she was dressed in a floral tea dress, her green eyes sparkling with happiness, she looked younger and happier than Melody had seen her before. The sadness that had been present in her eyes on their last visit had vanished completely.

They had spent the next couple of hours reminiscing on how their lives had changed, and all that they had been doing; as they made to leave, Melody promised Christina that they would stay in touch. Jack had pulled Christina to the side and shared a few private words with her, reluctantly joining them in Alex's SUV. The mood on the drive back to Jack's place had been so different, a new energy seemed to spark off him.

Melody's mobile phone alert brought her out of her reverie. Picking it up, she looked at the text message scrolling across the screen, "hey hun, have a fun time tonight, love, Linds". Another text popped up from Alex. "Hey babe, miss you x". Replying to them both, she sighed contentedly, deciding to head in and make a quick call to Sarah. Half an hour later, she hung up the landline; Sarah had been in a great mood, chatting excitedly about the trip she was going to be making to London on Sunday with a few of her and Lucy's friends to see the maritime parade of a thousand boats on the river Thames, a fact that it was just one of the many festivities being held for the queen's diamond jubilee, Sarah recited as Lucy's excited voice in the background informed her that she would be wearing her red, white and blue jubilee scrunchie making her smile. With Sarah promising to take loads of photos, she had said goodbye to them both.

It had been so good to hear them both happily planning their trip, the feeling of excitement rubbing off on her.

Heading up to her room, she showered and changed into cream cotton capris and a blush pink shirt, leaving her face free from makeup and her hair down; she slipped on her matching blush pink canvas pumps and headed downstairs. Making sure Toby had water and enough toys to keep him occupied, she grabbed her bag and mobile phone, locking up the cottage and setting the alarm, she headed out to the car and to her hair appointment.

Alex stared at the text from Melody, "miss you too, can't wait till I see you tonight", a line of four kisses making him smile.

"Everything okay"? Joel's voice broke the spell.

"Yes, so we're all set"? His voice was brisker than he had meant it to be.

"Yes, everything has been checked and double checked. All you need to worry about now is turning up", Joel teased as Alex thoughtfully rubbed the velvet box containing the emerald necklace.

"Having second thoughts"?

"Just a bit", Alex sighed, the feeling of the weight of the world on his shoulders.

"It's going to be fine, we've all got your back, just try to relax".

Grunting he picked up the box, "I've just got to make a quick stop before I head home, you'll be okay to lock up here"?

"Sure Alex, just got to make a couple of calls and I'll be heading off myself".

Turning back to look at Joel, he asked, "Have we any updates from Peter"?

"Still no movement on the place", Joel grimaced, adding, "that Tim fellows probably just given up by now".

"I don't think so", Alex scowled, a feeling of unease gripping him.

Leaving Joel at the office, Alex headed to his car, the velvet box now safely stored in his briefcase. They would be ready if he did make a move, each of their security men had a full description of Tim Abbott now, he mused, relaxing a little at the thought. A quick stop at the jeweller's and then home, he thought, smiling to himself at the thought of finally seeing Melody in her gown.

Timothy stared at his reflection in the mirror, his hair now bleach blonde had gone a shade lighter than it had stated on the packet, grabbing a pot of gel, he applied it to his short new haircut, spiking the ends till he was satisfied he had got the look exactly right. Grabbing the uniform and name badge, he dressed quickly, a sly smile spreading over his face as he looked at his reflection. "Well Owen, you look damn good even if I do say so myself". Checking on the drugged Owen one last time and finding him still slumped on the bed where he had left him, he chuckled to himself. "Sweet dreams, mate". On impulse, he grabbed Owen's car keys and left the apartment; he headed over to Owen's beat up ford fiesta, "this will do nicely". Jumping in, he started the car and headed for the Crafton hotel.

Melody made her way carefully down the stairs, the full tulle skirts of her gown brushing against the wall and banister; after having her hairstyle done at the salon, she had spent the rest of the time getting herself gala ready, the delicate scent of the perfumed body lotion she had rubbed in all over her body enhancing the light spray of perfume she had applied later. Stopping at the end of the hall, she watched as the front door opened. Alex stood in the doorway, dressed in an immaculate black tuxedo, his crisp white shirt pleated down the front, a black bow tie and cummerbund finishing the devastatingly handsome look, his black leather polished shoes gleamed in the evening sun. His hair slicked back with just a touch of brylcreem, making it look darker than normal, his strong clean-shaven jaw in profile as he turned to look at her; taking a step towards him, she felt the air almost crackle with their unspoken attraction.

Alex stood stock still, his eyes settling on Melody, a pure vision of loveliness. The rose-pink gown enhanced her beautifully soft looking skin, the tantalising hint of cleavage just visible above the sweetheart neckline, her long neck bare and begging for his kisses, wisps of hair spiralling down each side of her face, tiny diamantes glinting in the mass of pinned up curls. As she gracefully walked towards him, he caught the soft smell of flowers intoxicating his senses, the tulle skirts swishing silently as she came to a stop in front of him.

Her sultry eyes smiled shyly up at him, the amber in them glinting warmly.

"You look beautiful", he muttered, his own voice sounding strange to him; reaching out, he placed his hands around her tiny waist and pulled her close. "So beautiful", he moaned, placing hot kisses on her exquisite neck.

"You're looking pretty dashing too", she gasped, trailing her fingers over his broad chest as he nipped at her earlobe. Stepping out of his embrace, she looked up at him, "did you bring it"?

"Yes", his gruff voice betrayed his emotions as he pulled out the black velvet box, snapping it open. He turned her away from him and placed the emerald necklace around her neck, lingering longer than necessary as he fixed the clasp.

The necklace felt cold against her hot skin, turning slowly, she showed him the finished look, "will I do"? Her voice was hesitant as she fingered the heavy necklace.

"You're just missing one thing", he smiled, retrieving another smaller velvet box from his jacket and handing it to her.

Opening the box, her fingers shaking, she gasped as she saw the pear drop diamond earrings nestled inside. "Oh Alex, they're beautiful, did Christina lend these too"?

She looked up at him, her eyes questioning. "No, these are for you to keep, I wanted to buy my girl something special".

"Oh Alex, thank you", she sighed, as tears filled her eyes.

"Now, no crying, minx, can't have you ruining your lovely makeup", he teased, helping her fix the earrings in. "Now milady, your carriage awaits". Bowing gallantly, he stepped aside for her to leave. Grabbing her clutch bag, she swept past him, waiting while he locked the cottage.

"No horse and carriage, Alex", she teased, as they made their way to his SUV.

"I'm afraid the horse and carriage are in the shop, I hope milady won't mind roughing it a bit in this old metal carriage", he played back, opening the door for her and helping her inside.

Pulling up outside the Crafton hotel and handing over the keys to the valet, Alex made his way around to the passenger side and helped Melody out. Her eyes wide as she took in the stunning effect of the transformed hotel, fairy lights twinkled everywhere; a red carpet ran from the wide entrance stairs to the walkway. 'Hopes & Dreams' banners flanked each side of the massive open doors, music filtered out to them as other guests made their way slowly up the carpet, stopping often for the news reporters' photos.

Placing her hand in the crook of his elbow, Alex escorted her up the path, occasionally stopping to greet someone he knew. Scanning the crowd, she saw several security men dressed in black, their only give-away the small earpieces. As if he felt her tension, Alex leaned down. "Smile love, it's okay", he whispered, his breath tickling her ear. Standing taller, she pulled her lace wrap tighter together over the necklace, keeping it hidden as she posed for the cameras and then was swept inside. If the outside had dazzled her, she was not prepared for the inside; strategic lighting lit up the stone walls, bathing the whole area in a warm yellow glow. The foyer was packed with women all dressed in satin and tulle of varying shades, the men all dressed in tuxedos. Waiters hovered with trays laden with flute glasses of champagne; grabbing them both a glass from a passing waiter, Alex handed her one, taking a sip, she felt the bubbles explode in her mouth.

"Alex darling", a rather tall curvaceous woman called over to them. As she sashayed over, Melody noted the way her black satin dress clung to her every curve, her red dyed hair draped over her bare shoulder. "You've been keeping this pretty creature to yourself", she crooned, running a critical eye over Melody.

"Cynthia", he smiled, his irritation barely concealed. "Melody, may I introduce Cynthia Dowling, Cynthia this is Melody Croft".

Looking at Cynthia, Melody quickly realised that she was older than she had first appeared, her heavily made up face had fooled her from afar, but the wrinkles around her eyes couldn't be concealed closer up; her cold bejewelled hands grabbed Melody's "lovely to meet you dear", she smiled but her eyes remained on Alex.

"So, is Winston with you tonight"? Alex enquired, looking about the crowd for him.

"Oh, he's over there somewhere", she waved her hand, "schmoozing with some of his business associates". "So, tell me Melody, do you just hate these things as much as I do", she purred, linking her arm through Melody's.

"I can't say that I do, having not been to one before tonight", Melody shrugged.

"Oh goody, a newbie, well let me tell you who's who", promptly falling into a discourse of all the guests and their partners.

Alex leaned in and whispered, "I'll go check in with Joel, will you be okay here"? Nodding her head, she watched as he strode away, he was easily a head taller than most men in the room.

"Divine, isn't he", Cynthia gushed, bringing her attention back, "worked on our security at Winston's charity event last year, never could understand how he was still single, I'd keep an eye on that one if I were you". Smiling politely, Melody excused herself, there was only so much she could take of Cynthia's gossip. Walking over to the ballroom she peered inside, dining tables filled the room, lights threw orbs over the walls and floor; at the far end a stage was set, no doubt for the entertainment and then the live auction. "Beautiful, isn't it", turning around, Melody found herself looking at an older lady, her yellow silk gown understated, steel grey hair swept up in a chignon, a simple string of pearls and matching pearl stud earrings her only accessories. Soft grey eyes looked back at her, finally somebody real, Melody thought, feeling guilty at her uncharitable thoughts.

"It sure is", she smiled, relaxing for the first time that evening.

"I'm Rose and you are"?

"Melody", she smiled.

"Well, it's lovely to meet you Melody. I must say your dress is exquisite, is it a Dior"?

"Oh no, it's a vintage dress with a touch of my handywork", Melody grinned, touching the lace on the bodice.

"Well, my dear, you certainly have a talent, I would have sworn it was a Dior". Chatting for a while, Melody finally felt at ease. "I think that young man over there is trying to catch your attention". Rose inclined her head towards Alex, who was steadily making his way over. Spying a waiter, Rose bade her goodbye and headed over to him; as she watched her go Melody frowned, was she imagining it or was the waiter staring at her.

"Pull yourself together, he's probably just doing his job", she mentally chastised herself.

"Having fun"? Alex drawled as he finally reached her.

"Just meeting the locals", she laughed, all thoughts of the waiter gone.

"There's someone I'd like you to meet, I promised him an exclusive photo of you and the necklace". Taking her arm, he led her across the crowded room to a group of men. "Joe, this is Melody Croft, Melody this is Joe Lawson, he ran the story of the missing heirloom". He was shorter than Alex, his tux fitted tightly over his stout frame, his ruddy face beaming at her, his wavy peppered hair and silver framed glasses giving him a wise appearance as he thoughtfully stroked his clipped beard. Melody held out her hand, he took it placing a kiss on her knuckles.

"Lovely to finally meet you", he beamed "and this is the famous heirloom", he flicked a look at it, "if it's okay with you, I thought we could get a couple of shots by the lions", he indicated to the far wall, where two white regal stone lions sat on each side of large doors, each door draped with the 'Hopes and Dreams' banners. Wandering over, he positioned her in the middle, calling out instructions as he snapped several photos, "perfect, now slightly to the left".

Melody felt herself blush as other guests gathered around watching the photo shoot, "place your hand on the lion, and turn slightly to the right", he instructed as she got into position.

"That's it perfect, I think we've got it". Lowering his camera, he walked over to her, retrieving a notepad from his jacket pocket. "So let me check Melody Croft and you run Simple Crafts", she inclined her head, unfolding a piece of paper he leaned in, "just need your signature here", he indicated handing her the pen, "just a release form for the photos so I can't get the paper sued", he laughed as she signed her name. Taking the paper, he tucked it into his pocket. "Alex, a quick word if you don't mind", casting an apologetic look at Melody, Alex moved over to him.

"I'll be over there getting a drink", Melody sighed, disappearing into the crowd, grabbing a drink from a passing waiter, she headed to a quiet corner, the heat in the room becoming stifling. She took a sip of the cool champagne, watching the guests mill about, each wrapped up in their own little world.

Noticing Cynthia making her way over towards her, Melody quickly turned and headed away. Another tete a tete with her was the last thing she needed, placing her empty glass on a passing waiter's tray, she spotted Rose standing outside the gallery doors, an agitated look on her face. Deciding to check on her, she changed direction and headed for her. "Everything okay", she asked, watching as Rose wrung her hands in distress.

"It's my earring, I went in there to look at the paintings and noticed it's missing", she indicated to the room behind her and tugged at her bare earlobe, "I think it came out in there, but without my glasses, I can't seem to see it, my husband will be so cross with me", she sniffed, her eyes filling with tears.

"Come on", Melody soothed, opening the door and slipping inside, "I'm sure if it's in there, I'll see it". Following her inside, Rose closed the door behind them.

"I went over to the far wall first", she murmured, pointing down the room, Melody headed down the room searching the floor as she went, bending down she searched around the feet of a side table, if it was here, she was sure she would find it.

Feeling something cold settle on her bare shoulder, Melody turned her head to look, a silver lion head rested menacingly there glinting in the overhead lights; where had she seen that before she couldn't remember. Slowly rising up and turning, she saw that it was attached to a cane, a cane that Rose was holding, her soft grey eyes now hard, as she gazed at her with contempt.

"R-Rose", she stuttered questioningly as she took in the sight of the cruel tilt of her lips. Her eyes were now staring at the necklace, as she raised the cane, pointing it threateningly at her.

"I believe that is mine", she snarled.

"I d-don't understand", stuttering, Melody looked in horror at Rose, her face now contorted and evil.

"It's quite simple, you foolish girl, that emerald necklace is rightfully mine", raising up her hand, her fingers claw like, she reached out to Melody's throat.

Stepping back, Melody nervously glanced at the doors as one opened and a waiter appeared.

"Help", she cried out, her voice strained. He closed the door, hovering a moment, before walking up to them and snatching the cane from Rose's hand.

"Ah Timothy, so good of you to join us". Rose's voice boomed, now sounding icy and controlled.

"I think she's g-gone mad", Melody stuttered, looking at the waiter, his name badge clearly stating his name was Owen. Turning to look at Melody, the same contempt was written across his face.

"Aunt Primrose, I think this little miss thinks you're mad", he scornfully laughed. "I see you are wearing our heirloom", he spoke, lifting the cane and pointing it at her throat.

"I don't understand", Melody repeated, gasping as the nightmare of the lion headed cane started to resurface, "this is Christina Trafford's necklace, she lent it to me", her voice barely a whisper as a chill ran down her spine, surely this couldn't be the thief Tim Abbott, his hair was lanky brown not spiky and blonde. But why had she called him Timothy. "Who are you"? She asked, turning accusing eyes at him.

"I think she's starting to get it", he growled taking a step towards her. "Timothy Trafford, also known as Tim Abbott", he bowed mockingly, "and you've already met my Aunt Primrose", he stood gripping the cane, his eyes full of hatred.

"Finish her Timothy, but get it right this time, unlike your father, don't leave this one to survive"!

"Your father tried to hurt Christina"? She cried out, stalling for time, "w-why would he do that"?

"That heirloom should rightfully have gone to us, my brother Philip planned to take it on her birthday, but that little chit had hidden it, now finally it will be ours".

"That's right, father was too weak to finish what he started, but I'm not". Timothy advanced towards her raising the cane, snatches of the nightmare came rushing back to Melody as the lion headed cane glinted menacingly.

Primrose stepped back a few paces, her face contorted in rage. "I tried to be there for her after Philip failed his task, but she claimed to have amnesia and was always so damn secretive, always scribbling in those journals of hers". Pacing back and forth, her ranting continued. "When father got unjustly cut off from the family, I decided that one day we would bring them down and take what was rightfully ours, it was a long game and one I very nearly gave up on, until Timothy here heard of the estate sale". Pausing, she stopped and stared at Melody. "The trunks, you see, I was sure would contain those journals and with them finally in our possession, the secret of the heirloom would be revealed, I was certain she would have unconsciously left some clues to that night".

Melody stared from Rose to Timothy, her hands trembling as the realisation of the situation sank in.

"Did you send that thief to break-in to my cottage", her voice a mere croak, as the gravity of their intentions left her feeling weak.

Primrose tutted, "of course, and you just happen to be in the way. Now, Timothy, get it first, I don't want her common blood on it", she ordered. Reaching out to her, his clammy hand gripped her shoulder as he fumbled at the clasp.

"Please don't do this", Melody begged as the necklace slipped from her neck.

"If you had just left the last journal in your damn cottage for me, you wouldn't be in this mess right now, but you had to go and complicate things, didn't you", he scorned, prowling over to his aunt, he dropped the necklace in her claw like hands. So he was the thief; she couldn't believe she had been so easily duped, if only she could reach the doors and Alex.

Turning to run, Melody only made it a few steps as she felt the impact of the lion head as it crashed down on the back of her head; falling to her knees, she waited for the next inevitable blow. The sound of wood splintering from somewhere far off gave Melody a few precious moments to crawl further away. "I'm so sorry Christina", she breathed as blackness enveloped her.

Waking in an unfamiliar darkened room, the pain in Melody's head throbbed. She tentatively touched the spot, wincing as her fingers probed at the bump, it was sticky with blood but she was alive. She tried to sit up, the room spun as strong hands eased her back. "It's okay love, I've got you", Alex's voice soothed her as she slipped back into unconsciousness. Voices floated over Melody as she lay still, trying to gather her strength, slipping in and out of consciousness, was that Alex's voice? She tried to focus but could not seem to clear her mind. Someone was talking to her, bathing her head, the smell of the antiseptic cream making her feel nauseous. Slipping into blackness, she welcomed the oblivion it gave her.

Memories of Rose and Timothy stirred her. "The necklace, it's gone", she croaked, touching her now bare neck. Sitting up, she saw a large figure moving towards her, flinching back, she pulled at the covers.

"It's okay, it's just me", Alex's concerned face leaned into her.

"Oh Alex, they took it", she cried as he placed a glass of water to her lips.

"It's okay baby, we've got it". Placing the glass down and climbing onto the bed, he tucked her into his arms, cradling her, he stroked his hand against her cheek.

"It was Timothy Trafford; he was the thief", she gulped as fresh tears threatened to fall.

"I know, we've got him, now sleep baby, I'm here and I won't leave you". Alex looked down at her as she slept, the rage in him subsiding as the fear of nearly losing her took over. If she had died… he stopped, his thoughts going there, pulling her tighter to him, he breathed in her scent, her gentle sighs soothing him.

At least, he had had the jeweller's attach that listening device to the necklace, if not, he shuddered at the unfinished thought. He had nearly lost her twice, he damn well would not let another thing happen to her he swore. Melody snuggled into him, a small sigh escaping her lips.

"Alex", she whispered.

"I'm here love", he answered, resting back and brushing his lips against her forehead.

Looking around the hotel room, his eyes settling on her gown now draped over the chair, he felt his anger at Primrose and Timothy rise again. At least she was safe from them now, detective Frank Marsh had them both and with the recordings from the listening device, they would not be able to talk their way out of this one. Reassuring himself that the security guard posted outside the door would not let anyone enter the room, he rested his chin on her head and closed his eyes; from now on she was all that mattered to him.

Chapter 16

The days flew past in a flurry, baskets of fruit and flowers arrived en masse. Melody was overwhelmed by all the kindness. Susie had arranged cover for her at the shop, insisting that Melody take a week off to recuperate, which Alex had readily sided with. A quick call to remind Susie of their Wednesday delivery earlier had seen a tutting Susie telling her to "take a break and stop fretting, we got it covered". Smiling at the memory, she set about the task of opening another batch of cards that had been delivered that morning; she spied one from Christina and Jack, 'hope you are feeling better, looking forward to seeing you both soon' it read, smiling, she placed it down on the pile; they would be going to see them later today. Alex had insisted on her resting for days after the gala, promising her that they would visit and give them the necklace once she had recovered, and now with the bump barely visible, she had talked him into driving them there today. Glancing at her watch, she grabbed her phone and jumped-up, startling a slumbering Toby. "It's okay Tob's, relax", she laughed, heading up the stairs. Alex would be here soon, just enough time for a quick shower and a change of clothes, she mused, busily collecting her bathrobe and bits.

Dressing in a white mid-calf slip dress, the tiny green flowers dotted all over making her feel summery and fresh, straightening the frills around the sweetheart neckline, she tied the string in the middle of her bust into a bow. Leaving her hair down, she applied a little sage green eye shadow and black mascara; satisfied with the look, she powdered the freckles over her nose. A light spray of perfume and she was done. On impulse, she picked up the lip gloss and swiped a little onto her lips. Hearing Alex arrive, she stuffed her feet into her white canvas pumps and headed down to greet him.

Arriving at Christina's, a smiling Anne showed them through to the sun room where Christina and Jack sat waiting for them, pot plants grew vigorously throughout the sunny room reminding Melody of a jungle, a whirring fan above them gently rustling the leaves, cane furniture dotted around the room, a cane and glass coffee table sat in the middle, a tea set and a full matching double tiered cake plate set out for them all, rising up from a high backed cane chair, Christina rushed over to them, hugging Melody tightly.

"I'm so glad you came", she greeted them as Jack shook Alex's hand. Taking a seat on the two-seater, Alex turned to pull Melody down beside him. Pouring them tea, Christina placed it beside them and turned to sit back down next to Jack. "I must say I never would have believed cousin Primrose would have been behind all this", Christina gestured helplessly. "I'm so sorry you got dragged into this craziness".

Jack placed his hand over Christina's, "it's okay love, I'm sure they don't blame you".

"Of course we don't", Melody sighed, the last person she would have ever blame was Christina.

Alex leaned in, his expression tight. "Detective Lawson tells me they have enough on them to lock them up for an awfully long time, they won't be hurting anybody again". Reaching into his jacket pocket, he pulled out the black velvet box. "This belongs to you", he passed the box to Christina.

Lifting the lid, she stared at the necklace. "So much hurt over such a silly thing", she whispered placing it on the coffee table.

"I had the jewellers remove the listening device, you would never even know it had been there". Alex shifted uncomfortably in his seat.

"How clever of you to have thought about having it put there", Christina praised unconcerned if it had damaged the necklace, "quick thinking like that probably saved Melody's life", turning to Melody, tears filling her eyes, she repeated, "I'm so sorry my dear".

Shaking her head, Melody soothed "it's okay Christina, no-ones to blame except them".

"So tell me, how did that scoundrel Timothy get past your guys", Jack asked Alex, his voice raw with emotion.

"He stole the identity of a waiter named Owen, drugged him and changed his appearance to match Owen's, while we were looking for a man with brown lank hair, he slipped in under our surveillance with his short blonde spiky hair and stolen identity", Alex growled, a frown settling on his face.

"And this Owen, is he okay"? Christina spoke softly, recognising Alex's guilt at having missed Timothy's crafty disguise.

"Yes, he was found by his sister and taken to hospital, fortunately he had only managed to drink a little of the drugged whiskey, anymore and we would probably be looking at a murder charge". Christina's face paled as the horror of what could have been washed over her.

"I'm afraid there's more bad news", Alex spoke quietly, looking from Jack to Christina, "it came to light that Philip, your cousin was the one who attacked you on your eighteenth birthday" pausing for breath, he leaned in adding, "detective Lawson says he's looking into it but he probably won't be tried for it, as he's in a nursing home with dementia".

Christina's eyes filled with fresh tears, "I got a call late last night", she sniffed dabbing at her eyes, "the nursing home informed me that he died peacefully in his sleep yesterday evening. I knew he was obsessed with the necklace, but I never imagined for one moment he would have…" her words trailing off as a soft sob escaped her.

Jack moved closer to her handing her his handkerchief, "don't waste your tears on him my love", he soothed, stroking her hand gently. Melody watched as they shared a loving look, at least they had each other now, she mused, feeling her eyes fill with unshed tears.

The drive home was silent as both she and Alex digested all that had gone on at Christina's, the fact that Christina had told them that she would be donating the emerald necklace to the 'Hopes and Dreams' charity seemed fitting; Melody could understand not wanting to have it around, it seemed so tainted by all that had gone on because of it. If not for the heirloom, Jack and Christina would have not been parted for all these years. Fingering the bump on her head, she winced at the thought of what had nearly happened to her because of the necklace.

"Is it hurting", Alex's concerned voice broke her reverie.

"No, I was just remembering", she sighed, turning to Alex. "It's all going to be okay now Alex", she soothed, trailing a finger over his clenched jaw.

"If anything had happened to you, I'd never forgive myself", he grimaced, staring intently at the road.

"Well, it's all okay, you rescued me once again", smiling, she trailed a finger down his neck, "my handsome knight".

"All yours, milady", he gave her a lop-sided grin. Yes, he thought to himself, she was safe and the future was bright and all theirs for the taking.

Chapter 17

Saturday morning seemed brighter today, Melody thought as she got ready for Lucy's birthday party. For the past week, Alex had been so extra caring, taking on all of her chores, fixing them meals, barely letting her raise a hand, running Lucy's dress over to Sarah while she rested at home, he seemed to be keeping close by her and when he had to leave, he would always check that she had everything she could possibly need. He had even started taking Toby on his morning runs every day to make sure he was well exercised. She knew he blamed himself for not protecting her but gradually she had worn his barriers down, and the sparkle was finally back in his gorgeous grey-blue eyes. The fact that he had told her he loved her regularly still brought tingles to her skin, she loved him too she could not imagine her life without him now.

Smiling at her reflection, she pulled the brush through her hair, the cut on the back of her head now healed but still tender, the bump having long since gone, she slowed the brush strokes over it. Deciding to wear it down, she pulled the sides up and placed a butterfly clip in. She was really looking forward to Lucy's party, all their friends would be there too. Sarah had insisted the adults deserved a party too, and Melody had happily helped plan the event, albeit from the comfort of her sofa. It would be great to catch up with them all, she leaned into the mirror, applying her makeup, the soft apricot eyeshadow understated for the occasion, sweeping a black liner across her eyelid, following the lash line, she made a flicked wing at the end, adding mascara, the look enhancing her long lashes. Dabbing a little apricot lip gloss on her lips, she pouted at her reflection.

Pleased with her overall look, she headed to her wardrobe, selecting a white pair of capri pants, and a sheer apricot blouse, its colour enhancing her tan perfectly, grabbing a spaghetti strap t-shirt in white to wear underneath the blouse, she dressed carefully avoiding getting her makeup on the clothes. Slipping on her white canvas pumps, she strolled over to her full-length mirror to inspect the look, casual but smart, she acknowledged puffing her cheeks out. "You'll do", she sighed, spraying a little perfume on her pulse points.

Sitting in the kitchen a while later, gazing at Lucy's present all wrapped up, she remembered the porcelain doll, heading to her craft room she retrieved it, with its new outfit now a replica of Lucy's party dress, the bows in its hair the same ones Lucy would be wearing. She had procrastinated all week on whether to take it today, biting her lip she decided to take it. "I'm sure she will love it", she mused remembering Alex's reaction to it. Smiling at the thought of Alex's aversion for the doll, 'men' she muttered, rolling her eyes, her mind made up, she headed with it back to the kitchen, sitting the doll on the table, she went into the front room to get some wrapping paper and tape. "Might as well wrap it up", she laughingly told Toby as when re-entering the kitchen, she caught him eyeing the doll warily, "and don't you start that again", she wagged a finger at him sending him back to his bed.

Walking into Sarah and Lucy's home, the party well under way, Melody and Alex made their way to the kitchen. "Melody", Sarah called out, rushing to greet her, throwing her arms around her as several pairs of eyes turned to them.

"Aunty Mel", Lucy squealed in delight, joining the hug as she wrapped her arms around Melody's legs.

"Hey munchkin", she smiled, reaching down to Lucy. "Enjoying your party".

Turning her face to Melody, she grinned, "Yep, and I got some new crayons too, look", she pointed proudly to the small table where her friends sat drawing a box of a hundred crayons sat open.

"Oh, I hope I'm going to get another picture", Melody laughed, handing her the two presents. "These are from me and Alex".

Ripping the wrapping paper off, Lucy clapped her hands in delight, "look mummy, my very own makeup". Picking up the pink princess makeup box, she showed it to her mum, delightedly picking out little pots of sparkly eye shadows and lip-glosses. "Can I put some on, please mummy".

Taking the box, Sarah crouched down, "of course you can sweetheart, but how about you open aunty Mel's other present first".

Rushing back, she carefully opened the other present, her eyes widening in surprise as she saw the porcelain doll, "she's wearing my party dress", she laughed delightedly, hugging the doll to her, turning to Melody, she announced, "I'm going to call her Lulu, cos she matches me".

"Now Lucy, what do you say"? Sarah laughingly admonished, rushing at Melody and Alex, she threw her arms around their legs. "Thank you aunty Mel". She looked up at Alex, a cheeky grin on her face, "thank you Uncle Alex". Joel's bark of laughter rang out loudly, making everyone turn to him.

"Uncle Alex would probably like to play tea parties with you, Luce", he pointed at her new tea set still in its box, Charlotte's elbow jabbed into his side, stopping his teasing midway.

"How about we show aunty Mel your new bike", Lindsey suggested, diverting the attention from a rather awkward Alex.

Leaving Lucy in the garden playing with her new bike, Melody strolled back into the kitchen and over to Sarah. "She seems happy", Melody smiled.

"She is, and getting spoilt too", Sarah gazed lovingly out at her daughter and her friends as they played with Toby and Rex, "not sure how long the dogs will put up with that though", she laughed as they watched the girls dressing the tolerant dogs up in hats and sunglasses.

"How's the new job going"? Melody asked stepping back to look at her sister, drying her hands on a towel, Sarah looked up, a broad smile on her face.

"Oh Mel, it's wonderful! I feel so alive, I've picked it up quickly, they are sending me on a part-time computer course this September, and I might even try out a photography course, I've always had a thing for it".

Grabbing Sarah's hands, she squeezed them excitedly, "I remember when we were kids, you always had some kind of camera attached to you, snapping shots of bugs and stuff", grimacing at the memory of Sarah's childlike voice instructing her to 'hold that leaf carefully, don't let the bug fall off', while she zoomed in for the shot.

"I think I have an album of those photos somewhere around", Sarah sighed, heading to the bookcase full of photo albums.

"Um, I think I'll give it a miss", Melody laughed, escaping into the front room to find Charlotte.

"Coward", Sarah called out, her laughter following her as she headed away.

"Who's a coward"? Charlotte enquired as Melody sat down beside her.

"Oh, just me for not wanting to look at photos of bugs", laughing at the puzzled look on Charlotte's face, she added, "don't worry it's just a sister thing". Sitting back, she fixed her gaze on Charlotte. "Something's different with you", she tilted her head, trying to place what it was.

"It's my hair, Mel", she fingered her short blonde hair, the absence of her usual brightly coloured spiky tips suddenly registering with Melody.

"No pinks or blues today, huh".

Casting a cautious look towards the door, Charlotte lowered her voice, "I just wanted to look more feminine today". Taking a closer look with fresh eyes, Melody noticed her subtle makeup and floaty dress, a softer gentler look. Her usual spikey hair now combed back in soft waves.

"It's Joel, isn't it"? Melody saw the confirmation in her friends' eyes; never before had Charlotte changed for a man, this must be serious, she thought smiling at Charlotte. "Love is in the air", she whispered as Charlotte cringed, blushing to her roots.

"What's with the blush, pixie"? Joel sat beside Charlotte, cupping her chin as her blush intensified. "Are you two talking about us"? He turned to grin at Alex as he sat beside Melody.

"Never question two gossiping ladies, Joel", his growl of laughter infectious as Lindsey appeared with a tray of drinks.

"What's the joke", she asked, putting the tray down on the coffee table.

"Just these two being wise guys", Melody laughed, rolling her eyes.

"Well, grab your drinks, and come into the garden, it's time for Lucy to blow her birthday candles out", Lindsey admonished, shaking her head at her best friends, glad to see them so happy.

Standing beside Alex, his arm securely wrapped around her waist, Melody looked happily at her friends and family as they all stood watching, whilst the children all sat excitedly around the trellis table as they sung happy birthday, the feeling that everything would work out for them all washed over her. Lindsey had finally gone on a date with Andy, Sarah had a new life with Lucy, even Charlotte had met her match in Joel; glancing at them, she smiled to herself as she saw the way they leaned lovingly into each other. Yes, they all seemed content, happily ever afters could happen, she mused, thinking of Christina and Jack's love story. As Lucy blew the candles out with Sarah's help, everyone clapped, bringing Melody out of her musings. With the cake served up to all the children, Alex pulled away from Melody.

"If I could have everyone's attention", he tapped his glass as all eyes turned towards him, she looked at him standing tall in his cream chinos, his pale blue shirt sleeves rolled up to the elbow, the muscles in his arms flexing as he raised his glass for everyone's attention. Licking her, lips she pulled herself together; no time for fantasies, she chided herself, tearing her eyes from his open neck shirt and the tantalising glimpse of his chest. Catching Joel winking at him, she turned her attention back to Alex, his grey-blue eyes twinkling as he gazed upon her.

"Melody", he started as a hush fell over the guests; dropping to one knee, he pulled a small box from his trouser pocket. "From the moment I met you, I was smitten", he paused, his expression turning serious, "I never realised I could love someone so much". The crowd sighed making him pause once again; Melody felt herself blush, as every pair of eyes seemed to be watching her. "Will you do me the honour of marrying me", he held the ring box up, its lid open, revealing a solitaire diamond.

Time seemed to stand still as Melody looked from his adoring eyes to the sparkling ring, the feeling of love so intense for him washing over her. "Yes", she answered, her voice thick with emotion. Rising up to his feet, he placed the ring on her finger and swung her up into his arms, lowering her quickly to passionately kiss her parted lips. A roar from the guests broke out as they finally drew back, the sound of champagne corks popping as a smiling Sarah filled everyone's glasses up.

"To the happy couple", she exclaimed excitedly, wiping away a few stray tears.

"To Melody and Alex", they all chimed in.

Alex glanced down at Lucy as he felt her tugging on his trouser leg. "Uncle Alex, Uncle Alex", she beamed up at him.

"Yes sweetie", he responded, crouching down to her level.

"Can I be a bridesmaid, please", she implored, her missing front tooth making her look cute as she hopped excitedly from foot to foot, her doll hanging from her hand. Glancing questioningly at Melody, he caught her slight nod of approval.

Turning back to her, he pulled one of her bunches playfully. "Yes sweetie, we would love you to be our bridesmaid".

Suddenly turning shy, she raced back to her mum. "I'm gonna be a bridesmaid, mummy", she announced grabbing Lulu her doll tightly to her and casting a shy look towards Alex.

"You'll get used to her", Melody laughed at the look of confusion on Alex's face.

"She sure is a whirlwind, I see a lot of you in her", he grinned, wrapping a curl around his finger and giving it a tug.

Joel sauntered up to them, a grin splitting his face. "Can I be your best man, Uncle Alex"? His imitation of Lucy's sing song voice making Melody giggle.

"Well, if you can promise me that you will behave yourself, then the job's yours", Alex chuckled, pulling Melody into his arms,

"And will Charlotte be the maid of honour"? Joel asked, a devilish glint in his eyes.

"Enough"! Alex growled, "you don't need any more encouragement on that front". Seeing Charlotte watching, he sheepishly grinned and headed over to her, leaving the newly engaged couple shaking their heads at him.

The double celebrations went on happily for the rest of the day; Melody sat on the garden swing, admiring her ring for the hundredth time that day.

"She really is a cute kid", Alex praised, sitting down next to Melody, "I think I owe one to Joel though, playing tea parties is not how I imagined spending the best part of an hour". He stretched his aching shoulders, it had been sweet watching him sitting on a tiny chair, his body all hunched up as he sipped imaginary tea from Lucy's tea cups. Every time he had thought he had finished, Lucy and her friends had insisted he had another, until finally, he had exclaimed if he had any more, he would burst, which had sent the little girls into peals of laughter and he had made his escape.

"You're so good with them, though", Melody confided, biting her lip to hold back her laughter.

"You think so, do you. Wait till we have a brood of nippers, then remind me how good I am with them", he teased, watching her blush; he loved the way she reacted so innocently to him.

"So, you do want kids one day then, Alex"? She leaned into him, a serious look on her face. She had always wanted children, but they had never really discussed the subject.

"Yes, I'd love children with you, but there's just one condition", he paused, looking deep into her eyes.

Melody felt like her world had come to a screaming halt, her eyes wide with concern, she nervously licked her lips. "And that is"?

"Just promise me one thing darling, no creepy dolls for our kids". Sagging with relief, she did not know whether to punch him or kiss him; the decision was taken out of her hands as he leaned in, his lop-sided grin disappearing as he kissed her with a passion she had never known existed until now.

Epilogue

20th April, 2013

Melody stood at the opening of the church, her simple bouquet of peach and white peonies held tightly in her hands; glancing down at her satin mermaid wedding dress, she wondered if Alex would like her in it, the sheer lace covered the low bodice, making her feel a little more confident. As her maid of honour, Charlotte and bridesmaid Lindsey, entered the building, she watched as their peach bridesmaid dresses disappeared from her sight. It would be Charlotte and Joel marrying next, she thought, as excited nerves of her own imminent vows began causing butterflies in her stomach. Her niece Lucy stood eagerly waiting to proceed her. Dressed in a miniature replica of the bridesmaids' dresses, a basket of petals ready to scatter was held tightly in one hand and petals ready to scatter in her other hand.

"You ready love", Jack's voice broke into her reverie, offering her his arm, a warm smile lighting his eyes. "I'm proud as punch to be giving you away". She looked into his teary eyes, so glad now that she had asked him to walk her down the aisle; he looked so dashing, his soft grey suit and peach cravat making his white hair distinguished looking. His soft blue eyes held hers. "They would be so proud of you, you know", he sighed, knowing how much she missed the presence of her mum and dad.

"Thank you, Jack", she placed a kiss on his soft cheek, "I'm ready". Nodding to Lucy to start the walk, the music started playing an instrumental version of Shania Twain's, "from this moment on". Jack pulled her veil into place; tucking her arm back into the crook of his elbow, he lovingly tapped her fingers and escorted Melody into the church.

As their song played, Melody glanced briefly at the full church, her eyes searching out Alex. As they finally settled on him at the altar, her step faltered. He stood ramrod straight, his blue-grey RAF service uniform enhancing the power of his strong body. He looked so handsome standing there, she reflected, wishing she could run to him. As he turned to watch her approach, she saw the tension leave him, a look of pure love transforming his face. Finally reaching his side, she took his hand that he held out to her; her nerves evaporating as his fingers wrapped around hers, giving her a gentle squeeze. She gazed up into his eyes as the final notes of the music finished.

Alex had watched as his angel had seemingly floated towards him, the tension he had felt melted away and now it seemed there was only the two of them here together. A vision in white satin stood before him, through the thin veil he could see her face, the love in her eyes evident. The urge to kiss her was ever present. A discreet cough from Joel brought his attention back to the present, as the vicar started the ceremony.

"You may kiss the bride", the smiling vicar announced, finishing the ceremony. Alex had waited for these five little words for what had seemed like forever. Raising her veil delicately, he looked deep into her eyes, dipping his head and capturing her full lips; the kiss started out tender, gaining in passion as he held her close to him. Reluctantly parting as the vicar's voice boomed, "ladies and gentlemen, may I present to you Mr and Mrs Knight".

Turning to their guests, Melody felt a lump rise in her throat; they were all here, friends and family. Jack had returned to his seat after giving her away, his hand now holding Christina's tightly, the friendship the four of them had made over the last year so precious, they were almost like parents to her now. Susie and her husband Dave sat smiling back at her, Sarah wiped tears away as she gave a thumbs up, her camera hanging around her neck ready for action, RAF friends of Alex and Joel dotted throughout the church, each smiling their approval. Joel had joined Charlotte, his hand resting protectively around her waist; who would have ever imagined Charlotte finally settled down and in love, a happy smile tugged at her mouth remembering Charlotte excitedly telling her he was going to be staying here permanently, his plans to relocate back to the city no longer what he wanted. Shifting her gaze over to Alex's family, she smiled; they all sat smiling proudly at them. Her family now, she sighed, a feeling of contentment washing over her.

"Mel", Alex whispered close to her ear. She turned her head to him. "I love you darling", his lopsided smile she loved so much, caused havoc with her pulse, "now milady, let's go spend the rest of our lives together".

Please Review

Dear Reader,

If you enjoyed this book, would you kindly post a short review on Goodreads or on whichever store you purchased the book from? Your feedback will make all the difference to getting the word out about this book. Please also look out for my next book where Charlotte and Joel's story continues!

Thank you in advance.

About the Author

Growing up in the UK Samantha relocated to Ireland 28 years ago to be close to her parents, where she graduated from the IT with a business degree. An avid lover of writing, painting and animals she is always juggling new story ideas and a home full of very spoiled canines.